"How'd you pull the scam with the horn?" Mack asked carefully

He gestured to the unicorn lounging on the garage floor.

Picking up a clump of straw, Persephone scattered it evenly over the concrete. "Buster isn't a scam," she responded calmly. "I was there when he foaled. He came out with a little hump on his forehead. Of course, I wouldn't put it past Leo Ganders to try some kind of—well, call it surgical sleight of hand," she said with a wry smile. "But in this case fakery is impossible, Mack. Buster's a real unicorn."

Mack rubbed the back of his neck, which seemed to have been tense since he'd run into Persephone. "Okay," he said gruffly, "who is Leo Ganders?"

"The man I used to work for as a veterinary technician. Leo is Buster's original owner. He wants to sell him for ten million dollars." She flared, "I couldn't let Buster be sold like a . . . a . . . an animal."

"Ten million dollars?" Mack was stunned. This situation was unbelievable. He'd just wanted to help a woman in trouble, and instead she'd made him an accessory to theft—of a *unicorn!*

Dear Reader,

What is more appealing, more enduring than *Cinderella, Beauty and the Beast* and *Pygmalion*? Fairy tales and legends are basic human stories, retold in every age, in their own way. Romance stories, at their heart, are the happily ever after of every story we listened to as children.

That was the happy inspiration for our 1993 yearlong Lovers & Legends miniseries. One book each month is a fairy tale retold in sizzling Temptation-style!

The month of May brings Kelly Street's *The Virgin & the Unicorn,* a mystical and heartwarming tale about two people fighting to save a real, live unicorn. Persephone Snow, the virginal heroine, believes she and her magical beast are safe hiding in her family's castle...until Mack Lord finds them. Her newfound hero makes her see that escaping from the world is no way to live, and shying away from him is no way to love.

In the coming months we have stories from bestselling authors including Gina Wilkins, *When It's Right* (*The Princess and the Pea*), Lynn Michaels, *Second Sight* (*The Ugly Duckling*), JoAnn Ross, *The Prince and the Showgirl* (*Cinderella*), and Bobby Hutchinson, *You Go to My Head* (*The Legend of Bacchus*).

We hope you enjoy the magic of Lovers & Legends, plus all the other terrific Temptation novels coming in 1993!

Birgit Davis-Todd
Senior Editor

P.S. We love to hear from our readers.

EC A
G

The Virgin &
The Unicorn
Kelly Street

Harlequin Books

TORONTO • NEW YORK • LONDON
AMSTERDAM • PARIS • SYDNEY • HAMBURG
STOCKHOLM • ATHENS • TOKYO • MILAN
MADRID • WARSAW • BUDAPEST • AUCKLAND

To my magical sister Maureen,
and our unicorn-loving niece, Melissa.

Many thanks to Barbara Norman of the
Winners' Circle Ranch in Petaluma, California,
for the opportunity to meet Lakeville Laddie,
the smallest stallion in the world.

Published May 1993

ISBN 0-373-25541-1

THE VIRGIN & THE UNICORN

Prologue

"I WON'T LET YOU DO IT."

"Persy," said Leo Ganders, "there's not a thing you can do to stop me. Sit down."

She continued to pace, a tiny, wrathful figure in pink denim overalls.

"I hate being called Persy."

"All right, *Persephone*, stop wrecking the pile of the carpet. It's brand-new. Damn thing cost me—"

"The carpet!" Persephone blew wispy bangs out of her eyes. She sat and leaned forward, gripping the arms of the chair. "And you bought a new security system and that trashy diamond your receptionist's been flashing. You've been planning this sale for months!" she accused. "Haven't you?"

"Yes," he admitted with uncharacteristic calm.

Persephone's stomach sank. Leo was so happy with the sale he was foregoing the emotional fireworks that were his favorite indulgence. The deal must be unbelievably favorable . . . to the one person in the world whose welfare he never forgot: Leo T. Ganders.

"You son of a bitch!"

Leo raised his graying eyebrows. "Swearing? Since when did Miss Squeaky-Clean start cussing?"

"I'm just getting started, you—"

"No, you're not. You're finished," he interrupted. "Take a look at the letterhead. Whose name is that at the top?"

He pushed a sheet of paper across his desk. She scowled and crossed her arms instead of touching the piece of company stationery. A rattling air conditioner produced a lukewarm puff, stirring the office's stale heat. The air current lifted a corner of the paper and revealed the words, Ganders, Inc., Breeding Exotic Animals Since 1970.

"I'm aware I'm just an employee, Leo."

"A valued employee. I gave you a job right out of that vet tech program you went through at junior college, didn't I? A kid with no experience. I think of you as a daughter."

"Bull. You hired me because 'no experience' meant you got competent help cheap. I stayed because—"

Because this breeding farm in the hills of southern California was out-of-the-way. No one knew her. She could work with animals—a dream since childhood— and go about the very serious business of forgetting the past. Animals were safe. They recognized her as a soothing voice and a kindly pair of hands. The miniature horses, Vietnamese pigs and tiny goats didn't remember old scandals or headlines.

"Well, sweetie cakes?"

"It's none of your business why I've stayed. And don't call me sweetie-anything. Until last spring you didn't know I was alive. I was another underpaid, invisible veterinary assistant. It wasn't until Buster was born—" Her breath caught. "Not Buster. Please don't sell him, Leo."

"Maybe I gave you too much credit when that colt foaled. The vet would've got here eventually. Just because you delivered Buster, you think you're his mommy." He nodded knowingly. "I shouldn't have given you that bonus. It made you too big for your britches."

"I didn't get delusions of grandeur from a ten-dollar-off coupon for a manicure," she said witheringly. She held up her hands. They were small, like the rest of her. The nails were neatly pared and untouched by varnish. "Thank you very much but nail polish isn't my style. I gave the certificate to Gloria. She likes having her nails done because it sets off her diamond ring. I felt sorry for her because I figured the ring isn't exactly the pledge of fidelity she thinks it is."

Since Leo's pasty complexion couldn't pale, Persephone watched it turn green.

"If you've been filling Gloria with stupid ideas about that ring meaning an engagement or anything unrealistic like that—"

"Don't worry," she said, thinking she'd better not tell him his receptionist had started keeping bridal magazines in her desk drawer. "Believe me, I don't talk to her about your personal life. There are some things I'd as soon not hear. That's beside the point—"

He recovered his normal pallor. His bulbous eyes took on a gleam she didn't like at all. "Of course, I could maybe consider changing my mind about Buster if you're interested in what Gloria's been getting. You could give me a little incentive, see? We could get together...."

She stared at him in disbelief. What did he think she was?

"Leo," she said flatly, "I just said I'm not interested."

His tongue flicked over his lips. "Too bad you're frigid."

She gasped. It wasn't the first time in her twenty-two years she'd heard that opinion expressed by a man. But Leo's was the cruelest variation on the theme, and it hurt. How could men, even a pathetic excuse for a man like Leo, tell she'd never allowed anyone close enough to show her what love could be?

Warm color flooded her cheeks. "I'm not taking up your valuable time so you can insult me. Listen, I could handle you selling Buster to a breeder or a zoo. Why does it have to be this Chasmo character?"

"You can't believe everything you read in the supermarket tabloids," replied Leo. He tried to look noble. She noted he didn't do it very well. "Chasmo is an internationally acclaimed figure in the world of motion picture entertainment. An award-winning producer and director. He's well-known as a collector of unusual animals."

"Did you memorize that from his press releases?" she asked hotly. "The guy is also a world-class nut. You know as well as I do his private zoo is stuffed full of endangered species he's gotten illegally from all over the world. And he doesn't even take good care of them."

"I've been told those reports are exaggerated," Leo put in. "Buster could live out his days in luxury."

"Live out his days! You make it sound like he's ready to be put out to pasture. He's five months old! A baby!"

"So he'll have a chance to bond with his new owner. That's the word, right? Bond? Everybody will be happy. Buster'll be happy, I'll be happy, Chasmo will be happy."

She jumped up and started pacing again. "You'll be rich. Buster will be miserable, maybe even dead. Your Saint Chasmo has been cited twice for neglecting his animals. Did you know that?"

"He goes on location a lot. But you don't have to worry about Buster being left with nobody to watch him. Chasmo's going to bring the colt with him while he travels," said Leo.

"Oh, no." A suspicion struck Persephone and made her feel sick. "You can't be serious. He wants to drag Buster into his horrible action-adventure and disaster films, doesn't he? With all those earthquakes and buildings collapsing, and lights and crashing cars and explosions? Not to mention the noise. No wonder you've been keeping Buster's existence a secret. The animal rights groups would have your hide. Do you consider that an appropriate environment for a horse, especially one as sensitive as Buster?"

"Buster'll be famous. He'll be the biggest thing since Rin Tin Tin," offered Leo, confirming her deduction. "Would you deny him this opportunity?"

"It'll *kill* him. Safety doesn't come first on those projects. A couple of stuntmen died making Chasmo's last movie. Miniature horses are rare. And Buster isn't just any miniature. He's one of a kind. If something bad happens to him, there may never be another like him." She produced an argument that Leo ought to appreciate. "The stud fees are going to be enormous."

"If he breeds true," said Leo sourly. "You got any guarantees?"

"No, of course not, but—"

"I doubt the stud fees would match what Chasmo's offering. Ten million dollars is a lot of money for a horse that won't grow to be more than thirty inches high."

"Ten million?" Tears pricked behind Persephone's eyelids. Her boss would never have the gumption it took to turn down that kind of money.

The circumstances of Persephone's life had forced her to become an expert on moral courage. Leo didn't have any. She'd had to face that conclusion during her first month of handling the ranch's veterinary medicines and checking on the day-to-day health of the animals. Her boss had suggested she sign an invoice for fewer supplies than a pharmaceutical company had delivered. At her furious refusal to defraud the company, he had backed off.

The experience had made her hope there was a chance he'd retreat from the sale. No such luck, she thought. In the unlikely event Leo had an unsuspected reserve of integrity buried somewhere deep down, it was obvious he wouldn't expend it on Buster.

"Where's a hero when you need one?" she muttered.

"Huh?" asked Leo.

She sighed. "Never mind."

Leo wouldn't understand what she yearned for. A gallant prince, like the ones who ruled fairy-tale kingdoms where there were never unhappy endings. She wouldn't mind letting somebody—a big, brawny male somebody—convince Leo to change his mind. It wouldn't take much of a show of force. Leo had very little physical courage.

Persephone was used to fighting her own battles. She'd had to learn how. But right now it would have been a relief to call on some help. She toyed with the idea. A potential prince would have to be somebody strong who knew how to channel his strength. Handsome but not too handsome. Persephone had dated a really gorgeous man once, and come out of the experience convinced that model-perfect men couldn't be depended on. She didn't want anyone too vain to risk his precious skin or too self-centered to appreciate a woman's intelligence. This situation called for a real, sword-wielding, old-fashioned hero. Preferably one willing to follow orders.

She gazed out the window at a corral. The offices were located in a tired old mobile home that squatted among barns, sheds and pens. Gander's was a shoestring operation. Its regular method of running was to lease a few animals to the movies or television, and sell some to petting zoos or pet shops. The worn buildings and kempt corral looked the same as usual. In other words, no heroes waiting to rescue a denimed damsel in distress were hanging around.

The fencing of the corral was low, in keeping with the size of the horses it contained. Several of the animals stood peacefully in the not-yet-hot sun of the September morning. Out here in the hills, the smog from neighboring L.A. was only a smudge on the horizon. The blue sky almost sparkled. In the crystal air all the miniature horses—who would grow no larger than a good-sized dog—were creatures of enchantment. But one stood out.

Buster was the only one with a seven-inch corkscrew horn growing out of his forehead.

Why, despaired Persephone, had the Fates looked at an insensitive, uncaring schmuck like Leo Ganders . . . and given him the astonishing fortune to own a unicorn?

Not for the first time, she decided the Fates must be nearsighted.

Maybe it was time to correct their bad vision. A daring, scary idea sneaked up on Persephone. What if . . .

Leo picked up the phone and punched the interoffice button. "Gloria," he said, "I want you in here."

"About Buster—" Persephone began.

"Forget Buster, sweetie cakes. Just keep out of the way while he's turned over to Chasmo's people tomorrow. I don't want trouble."

The top of a peroxided perm poked through the door. Somehow Gloria's failure to achieve a natural-looking color always made Persephone self-conscious about the silvery blondness of her own shoulder-length hair.

"You want me, Leo?" asked the receptionist, cocking her head.

"Yeah. I want you." Leo spoke in what he seemed to think was a sexy growl. He glanced at Persephone. His smirk said, *See what you're missing?*

Repressing the impulse to offer Gloria sympathy, Persephone said hastily, "I'll be leaving now."

Leo didn't even look at his mistress, who was lowering her ample bottom onto his lap. "You do that, Persy. And don't forget—that unicorn is none of your business."

Persephone closed the door gently behind her and leaned against it. The decision she'd made about Buster scared her straight down to her toes.

She'd never stolen before. Honesty was the shining ideal of her life. It had been for five years, ever since the day she'd found out the truth about how her father had been able to afford the nannies and private schools that had insulated her childhood.

Seventeen was a vulnerable age. Right on the precipice of adulthood. A bad age to discover your dad had been able to treat you like a princess because he financed the swankiest prostitution ring in the Pacific Northwest.

"Blood will out," she murmured. "Especially bad blood."

She was no longer a disillusioned teenager, repulsed by sexual activity because it reminded her of the women exploited by her father. Her body was healthy and mature. To put it bluntly, she was ready for a man. Persephone was too familiar with animal biology not to recognize it. If the right guy were to stroll into her life . . . but he hadn't. Not so far.

The wall of the cheap office building had shiny plastic panels. Persephone stared at her reflection in one of them. Her pale, expressive eyebrows, elegant nose and willful mouth bunched together in a scowl. As the newspapers had mentioned far too often, they were the delicate, aristocratic features she'd gotten from her father.

Surely a little of the craftiness that had made her family rich flowed through her veins. With no false modesty, she knew she was smart.

After all, she had survived.

It hadn't been easy. There weren't any funds to inherit after Thomason Snow died of a heart attack on his way to jail; as the proceeds of crime, his fortune had gone to the state. The family's vacation home, a white elephant built of stone on the Oregon coast, where her late grandmother had once lived, was the extent of her inheritance. The place ate money. For a troubling number of years, she hadn't even been able to afford to pay all the taxes.

Nor had she lived there since the day of Thomason's funeral. Too many memories. Too much pain. Persephone had fled, and even though she'd never been raised to be anything but Daddy's pampered debutante, she hadn't done too badly.

She'd figured out how to dodge reporters until the Snow "heiress" was old news—and avoiding the vultures of the press was *hard*. A two-year veterinary technician program had followed. She had studied when she wasn't waiting tables for her tuition and rent money.

Running out of Leo's office building, she stepped off the rickety metal porch into the deserted yard near the corral. Taking someone else's ten-million-dollar unicorn couldn't be counted as terribly bright, but Persephone didn't care how stupid kidnapping might be. As Buster cantered toward her, her heart melted. The cream-colored colt crowded up to the fence for attention.

"Hello, sweetie. How are you today?"

He butted several fillies out of the way to get to her. The other horses danced out of reach of his horn, graceful despite their short legs and stocky bodies.

"Minis" had normal-sized ancestors. Their lack of height was the result of breeding by people curious to see just how small horses could get. Persephone found the breed, the American Miniature Horse, sweet-tempered and noncombative. The herd certainly had a healthy respect for Buster's mutation.

He propped his round chin on the rail and blinked liquid brown eyes at her.

"We're going to take a ride in Persephone's van. Would you like that? I'm taking you—"

Where could she take him? Her apartment manager wouldn't allow any kind of pet, not even a bird, let alone a beast like Buster. Besides, once Leo discovered that she and the horse were missing, her apartment would be the obvious spot to search.

She grimaced. There was only one place she could think of where Buster might be safe.

"I'm taking you home to Oregon," she said resignedly.

Best to get her unicorn-napping done as soon as possible, while Leo was . . . distracted . . . and the other employees were busy in different parts of the ranch. She lifted a bit from a peg. Buster took the metal mouthpiece trustfully, his velvet mouth nipping at her fingers in what felt like a kiss. The caress fueled her determination.

This idiocy was probably going to screw up her life forever, but she wasn't letting him be sold into a short and horrible existence that would be the horse equivalent of hell.

And that was that.

1

"UNBELIEVABLE," said Mack Lord.

He squinted at the "old Snow place." That's what the locals called it. Wreathed in the shifting fog of the Oregon coast, the gray stone house stretched up into the sky. Its outside walls gleamed with wetness. The air had a damp chill.

He shrugged his shoulders deeper into his bomber-style leather jacket, which was old bordering on ancient. Every now and then he considered getting a new one, but he never did. Its black cowhide was familiar and comfortable, the soft folds worn to the contours of his body. So what if it made him look a little too tough, like an ex-boxer? That was what he was. He was wise enough to wear a suit and tie when he mingled with the stockbrokers and bankers who helped him multiply his money. Image was important in making business go smoothly. Otherwise, he dressed to please himself. The jacket was an old friend, and he never forgot a friend.

Rarely did he make the mistake of accepting anything on appearances, either. He hadn't in his boxing days, before he retired. And he didn't now. The Snow estate was going up for sale. Unpaid back taxes. He had plans that required a large building out in the country. So he'd driven up from Portland to take a look at the place himself.

"I expected something big," he said to his companion. "But nothing like this."

His voice echoed. Surrounding him was an acre of— damn, once upon a time it must have been an impressive lawn. Some gardener's pride and joy. Now it grew wild. A variety of weeds towered waist-high. White ones dusted him with pollen. Purple-headed thistles caught at his pant legs.

A curving driveway cut through the former lawn. Untrimmed bushes and shaggy trees pressed in at the edges.

The house itself was huge and . . . eerie.

"Sure is a surprise out here in the middle of nowhere," said Joey, sticking his head out of the car window. Joey had been Mack's first trainer. Now in his sixties, he was Mack's "assistant." Decaying knee cartilage had forceably retired him from sports, and Mack liked the bald little man's company. "It's incredible," Joey went on. "Looks like it dropped from another planet."

"You're right about that."

A few miles to the south lay Rockaway, and to the north spread Wheeler, both of them the funkiest of beach towns. Oyster shacks, beachfront condos and frankly tawdry gift shops were the rule there. Pine-forested hills filled the space in between. The hills ended abruptly in steep, rock-strewn grades that leveled out into wide, flat sand. Beyond the beach came the ocean. Pewter-gray water constantly tumbled over itself in a race for land.

The Snow estate nestled in those green pines, on top of a cliff indistinguishable from a hundred others along the coast. At the cliff bottom ran another line of perfect beach. The same ocean poured itself toward the same shore.

But the stone fence around the Snow estate kept out the modern world. And kept in a world of the past.

On the Snow property, there wasn't a hint that people lived in rowdy beach towns nearby. Untamed, overgrown beauty thrived. The flowery white tops of the weeds waved in the cold breeze like ghostly arms. Anything could have been hiding in the brush that choked the woods circling the house. Anything.

An inborn wariness caused the skin on Mack's arms to prickle. He frowned. His eyes swept back and forth, seeking clues to his uneasiness.

Some people believed an ex-boxer-turned-businessman couldn't be overly bright. It was true that Mack often made judgment calls based on instinct. But, because he *wasn't* a fool, he always double-checked his conclusions against the facts.

The atmosphere here was so strong, it formed a fact in itself.

"Will you be all right on your own?" asked Joey.

Despite his own misgivings, Mack regarded the older man quizzically. "Think I can't handle myself?"

Joey regarded his boss.

Resigned to the inspection, Mack waited it out good-naturedly. He had no vanity about his looks. While his face didn't scare little children, his blunt features and hard jaw weren't handsome and he knew it. But he worked out regularly to maintain his big shoulders, flat abdomen and buttocks, and muscular legs—a classic boxer's build. His strength and quickness had gotten him into prize fighting. Luck, and intelligence, had gotten him out.

Joey chuckled. "I guess you can handle yourself."

"Let's hope so, anyway. I'll spend a quick hour going over square footage and checking the building for soundness. I want to figure out whether I want it, and if I do, what kind of bid to make on it."

"Isn't there an asking price?"

Mack flicked a finger through the papers on the clipboard he held. "Yeah, but that's just a minimum the state is prepared to accept. This is a back-taxes auction. The owner really blew it with this property. His name is—it's just an initial. P."

"Madeline in the office says that stands for Percy."

"Poor bastard," said Mack idly.

"You said it," Joey agreed. "What a name to hang on some unsuspecting boy."

"Percy must be in pretty dire financial straits. Imagine letting all this go for back taxes."

Joey scratched the bald spot on his head. "You mean he tried to cheat the government?"

Mack's eyes ran over the stone building in front of him. "Nah, as far as I know, the present owner hasn't done anything criminal. Percy just hasn't paid his property taxes. The old owner, his father—now that guy was a different story."

"Thomason Snow," said Joey. "I got to talking with the waitress in that seafood shack where we had lunch. She says he's practically a legend around here."

"Well, he kept his family rich off women's misery and men's foolishness for forty years."

"I heard his call girls were real high-class," said Joey in a wistful tone. "Real nice."

"We grew up in northeast Portland. You know as well as I do that prostitutes don't look glamorous when they're girls you went to grammar school with. They just look . . . sad. And they often die young."

The dying young part was, partly, what bugged him about Snow's business.

Boxing could have killed him long before his time. Before he walked away from the game two years ago, he was still winning all his fights, but recovery from each bout took longer every time he fought. Sometimes his ears rang. Looking at the immediate future, Mack had seen himself an old man...before he reached thirty. So he quit. It was a hard decision to make, because he wasn't a quitter. Stubbornness formed the bedrock of his nature. But he wasn't mule-headed enough to ignore the evidence his own body was giving him. He already held every title boxing bestowed on a heavyweight. And God knew he'd had enough of the lack of privacy that goes along with being a national celebrity.

At least the investments he'd made with his prize money were doing well, so leaving the boxing game didn't represent any financial hardship. Better a bored dabbler in the stock market than a punch-drunk wreck, reeling through comeback attempts. Far better.

The hearing problem had gradually cleared up. The ravages that were the usual reward of a career in the ring passed him by. More trophies wouldn't have made up for shot hearing, blurred eyesight, faulty balance, brain damage or early death. Especially early death.

In the meantime, he'd spent the last two years watching his money grow. There'd been a woman. It hadn't worked out. He made charity appearances, drawn more and more to do something for the kids who wandered the streets of his old neighborhood, looking for and, too often, finding trouble. The boys woke his angry sympathy. The girls broke his heart. Kids, just kids, falling into the hands of pimps . . .

"Thomason Snow was a taker, Joey," Mack said. "He wore his suit and stayed in his clean office and raked in the money women earned abusing their bodies."

"Kind of like promoters make fortunes off boxers, huh?"

"Exactly," agreed Mack caustically. "It won't hurt Snow's heir to give up a little."

Joey screwed up one eye to take a better look at the stone pile. "Little?"

"Yeah." Mack rubbed the back of his neck. "It's not a one-room hovel, is it? I need something big, but . . . geez."

The building was big enough to shelter dozens of runaway teenagers and street kids. However, at first sight the structure looked highly unlikely for any practical use. A shame, he thought. "The location's good— far from gangs and the kind of people who'd be a bad influence," he thought aloud. "But it's sure not what I had in mind. Joey, I need some time to think this place over on my own. Mind going sightseeing for a while? Be back by two."

He forgot the car before its exhaust faded into the air.

Mack tapped the clipboard in his hand against his thigh. The report clipped to it had lots of little boxes, all neatly filled in. The boxes told him the number of rooms, type of heating and sanitary arrangements, even the quantity of telephone jacks.

Unfortunately, the realtor who'd filled in the blanks had left out one significant fact.

"Damn it all, the thing's a castle," he muttered.

Turrets sprouted like mushrooms. The copper roofing was the color of seawater and the giant, hand-worked stones rose to a height of a hundred feet. He'd seen smaller department stores. Windows were few and narrow. Arrow slits? Holes for cannon placements? Maybe some long-dead Snow had had a premonition the family would need to hold off a siege.

Mack shook his head. Even money hadn't been able to save Thomason from a dicey heart. Apparently the shock killed the guy when the vice squad had finally moved in on him. And now Percy, the Snow heir, was losing a piece of the luxury made possible by Thomason's ill-gotten gains.

The Snows must have carted the building to America stone by stone from England or Europe. Or they ordered an architect to make it look as if they had.

A notice glued to the front door warned trespassers away. But he had a key, fast-talked out of the state controller's office.

The key opened the metal-banded door.

Musty air made him scowl with distaste. Sighting a wall switch, he flicked it on. Lights blossomed in dusty chandeliers, casting a muted glow over antique-looking chairs and side tables shoved up against the walls. Gilt frames surrounded paintings by famous artists. The pictures didn't look like prints, either.

None of the Snows' furnishings had been removed. The state had only recently taken possession.

The castle couldn't be used in its present state as a shelter. Reporters would have a field day complaining that street kids were living it up among Rembrandt paintings and Louis the Whatever-Number-He-Was chairs, while Joe Taxpayer couldn't afford a burger and fries.

Mack fingered his chin. Normally, he could care less what the press said. Unfortunately, he would need publicity to help raise the kind of bucks it would take to renovate this place into a usable shelter. He was prepared to drop a big chunk of his own money into the project. But it was going to take a bigger chunk.

Determination to make the shelter idea succeed hardened in him. It wasn't that he was a bleeding heart. If anything, those who knew him best called him too tough. But Mack had come from nowhere. He knew what nowhere felt like.

He checked his watch. "Might as well take a look around, now that I'm here."

Something about the place had him talking to himself. He rubbed the back of his neck uncomfortably, and realized this was the second time he'd done so. Something about the place . . .

Mack Lord had never thought of himself as sensitive. Yet something was bothering him right now. Either he had suddenly developed delicate sensibilities— which he didn't believe for a minute—or there really was a peculiar quality to this place. He could have sworn not-quite-human eyes were staring at him from a vantage point just out of sight or hearing by normal eyes, normal ears.

Mack checked his watch. There was almost an hour to kill. He hated wasting time. Always had. Perhaps it was the dislike of wasted time that was pushing him to do something concrete, something lasting, for street kids. He needed a challenge again.

The devil with psychic warnings. He didn't believe in that stuff, anyway. Raising his clipboard, he uncapped a pen with his teeth and got to work.

PERSEPHONE STEERED her battered yellow van toward the grocery store. Although the need to hurry pressed in on her, as it always did when she left Buster alone at the castle, once in the parking lot she dovetailed the van inside the lines carefully. The last thing she needed was a policeman insisting on seeing her driver's license. For all she knew, Leo had reported her to the authorities. Every cop in the state could have been looking for her in the month since she had taken Buster.

Picking out groceries was easy. She bought things that didn't require turning on the stove. It would be a disaster if an alert meter reader detected an increase in power usage at the castle. The electricity was on, heaven knew why. The only people who ever came around were men in suits with clipboards. They stared and scribbled and went away again.

None of them had looked closely enough to find Persephone. Or Buster in the lean-to she'd built in a tangle of bushes near one side of the castle. Or the room in the daylight basement she'd fixed up as a bedroom so she could be close to him.

She *assumed* the men were meter readers. On the chance they were detectives, sent by Leo to snoop around her old home, she avoided them. In fact, she avoided everybody who might remember her as a child summering in the vicinity. Persephone even did her shopping in Tillamook, a medium-sized town fifteen miles out of her way. No one would know her there.

Filling a cart took half an hour. The checkout line slowed her down. All the customers ahead of her seemed to have coupons or need a price check.

In racks near the checkout stands, tabloid newspapers displayed pictures of celebrities, their images frozen in harsh lights. She shook her head over the cruelty. Her own picture, young and blank-faced from grief, had once looked out at harried shoppers. Without pleasure she scanned the more outrageous headlines.

None of them mentioned a stolen unicorn, she noted. In spite of the relief that washed over her, Persephone's stomach rolled over.

She needed to control her thoughts better. When she didn't, the anxiety of remembering Leo and Chasmo and her career as a thief drove acid into her throat.

She was fairly certain there hadn't been any publicity about the kidnapping of the horse so far. Apparently Leo was still pursuing his policy of not publicizing the colt's existence. She imagined him perched on his hilltop, like a frog on a lily pad, waiting. Just waiting. If Buster came within his reach, he would snatch the unicorn back. Leo wouldn't wave goodbye to ten million dollars without a fight.

She glanced behind her in the line. Nobody looked much like a private investigator.

Not that she knew what one looked like.

Sometimes Persephone worried about what the month of self-deception was doing to her mental health. On the whole she coped more easily by pretending the way she and Buster lived was ordinary.

"Those tabloids are better than the comics," commented an old lady next to her.

Persephone jumped. She'd gotten out of the habit of talking to people. But if the blue-haired senior citizen beside her was a private eye, she'd eat one of the newspapers.

Smiling, Persephone said, "They are incredible, aren't they?"

Then her eye was caught by a more respectable periodical in the same rack. A headline read, Snow Castle Up for Sale.

"Oh, no," she said numbly. "Oh, no."

"Do you need to sit down or something?"

"No, thank you." Persephone grabbed the local magazine and read.

It was bad. Really bad. How could the state just sell the place out from under her? She'd been making payments. Not large ones, it was true . . . vet techs didn't make huge amounts of money. And property taxes in Oregon were sky-high. Had she sent anything the last time she'd received a bill? She couldn't remember. Apparently the government had decided to put the property up for sale to the highest bidder.

The magazine article in her hands made it sound as if it were only a matter of time—and not much time, at that—before the auction would be held.

Her turn in line came. She shuffled sideways until she was in front of the cash register, and kept reading.

"Miss, you gonna put the groceries on the checkout stand or what?" asked a gum-chewing clerk.

She tore her eyes away from the magazine. "I beg your pardon?"

"The groceries."

"Oh. Sure." One-handedly heaving milk, bread, vegetables and cold cuts out of the cart, she continued to skim the page.

No wonder the castle had been crawling with men in suits. God, where were she and Buster going to go? The number of places she could hide a three-quarters-grown unicorn were limited. Actually, they were limited to ... the castle.

"Miss? That's forty-eight dollars and thirty-five cents."

Blindly, she looked at the checker. Digging money out of her purse, she dropped it into his outstretched hand and pushed the cart out of the store.

How about Alaska? she thought. There was a lot of uninhabited land there. As she tumbled bags helter-skelter into the van, she wondered what she and Buster would live on if they had to run and hide again. An Alaskan winter would require survival gear. Not to mention basics like shelter of some kind and warmth and food. She'd withdrawn her life savings in cash the day she stole Buster and the money was holding out so far, but a major move would leave her broke.

Not just a little broke. Flat broke.

Driving with automatic competence, Persephone navigated out of Tillamook along the coast highway. A turnoff led to a little-used road that wound through a forest. The old monster she drove bumped over potholes and then onto the smoother surface of a dirt track.

Close to home, unreasoning panic flooded into her chest. She wouldn't feel reassured until she saw that Buster was all right. She leaned forward as she whipped the van around a corner with her foot pressed firmly on the accelerator.

A culvert at the bottom of the old formal garden was her entrance onto the estate. Her own personal rabbit-hole.

She jerked on the emergency brake, calling herself a fool. *Nothing's going to happen in the next two minutes. Unload the groceries, stupid, and then you can check on Buster.* Instead, flinging herself out of the seat, Persephone squeezed through a gap in the high stone fence and set out at a run for Buster's makeshift stable.

The garden formed an obstacle course of grabbing rose thorns and long chrysanthemum stems that caught at her ankles. There probably wasn't a creature on the property except herself and Buster, and a few birds and squirrels. But Persephone found herself hurrying as fast as she could.

Buster's stable, a lean-to of scrap wood and thatch, yawned empty.

"Oh, darn!"

Holding the stitch in her side, she looked around sharply. Adequate proof the unicorn had been there until recently lay in the fresh straw she'd put out that morning. Singlehandedly cleaning up after even a little horse was a major job. She took the chore seriously. Anyone who wandered through would be able to detect Buster's presence by his smells. Disposing of Buster's smells was a task she forced herself to perform several times a day.

It wasn't hard to track him; he was a charming but messy little beast. A rail lay knocked to the ground. Persephone stepped over it to follow his trail of "signs." Nibbled leaves and grasses also showed which way he'd gone.

A tuft of creamy hair hung on the splintered frame of the outside door leading directly into her room. She'd left it open to allow air to circulate. That had obviously been an unintelligent thing to do, since Buster had simply walked into the basement bedroom.

"Buster?" she called softly as she went through the door, jiggling the halter she'd grabbed from the lean-to.

A month of successful hiding had lulled her into letting down her guard on this one tiny detail.

And now she was paying for it.

2

AFTER GOING THROUGH the castle, Mack would believe anything.

The place was huge. In addition to more flights of stairs than he wanted to count and a wing of nothing but bedrooms, it had a kitchen left over from the Middle Ages with a fireplace an ox could be roasted in. Snow probably had. An ox or business associates who annoyed him.

The information sheets told him there was also a daylight basement kitchen with modern appliances. And servants quarters. He hadn't bothered to investigate those. His fifty-five minutes were almost up.

Back in the entry hall, Mack walked stiff-legged over the black-and-white checkerboard marble floor. Although he worked out the same way he did everything else, hard, that last flight of stairs had almost winded him. Getting old, he thought with disgust. Thirty-two was young for most people. It wasn't young for a boxer or for the mountain-goat athletics required to inspect the Snow castle in less than an hour.

After expending all that energy, the last thing he expected to find was an elevator. And yet, tucked under the main staircase, so unobtrusive he hadn't noticed before, there one was.

Granted, it wasn't much. All gilt and grillwork, the structure looked extremely rickety. However, assuming the damn thing worked, it would have saved him a lot of steps. More out of curiosity than anything else, he jabbed the call button.

To his surprise, the elevator hummed. It worked. Mack watched, fascinated, as the iron cage descended, clearly visible behind a wrought-iron safety grille. An electric bulb inside gave it the brilliance of a lighted stage.

Or the aura of another dimension.

As the cage lowered, tiny hooves appeared.

Mack did a double take and froze. The hooves were attached to spindly legs.

"How did you get here? And what kind of animal are you?" Mack asked. And what the hell was he supposed to do with it? "Not a dog, obviously. A goat? A very young pony?"

The swishing tail he glimpsed eliminated the idea of a goat.

"Okay, so you're a baby pony. A fat baby pony," he decided as more of the animal slid into view. He had a nice view of a wide rump and a barrel chest.

With a mechanical shriek, the grille opened. The hum of the elevator stopped. In the silence, the midget pony performed a turn.

"My God," breathed Mack.

The creature had a horn sticking out of its forehead. A bone-white protrusion that twisted like a giant screw. It ended in a wicked point.

A mane the color of ivory drifted over the animal's short neck and fell into brown eyes that showed a hint of white all around.

The unicorn whinnied at him. For the first time in his life, Mack understood the meaning of *horselaugh*.

A flicker of the light bulb was Mack's only warning that the elevator was ready to move again. He hurled himself forward to stop it. Too late. The grille closed. He stopped short as the cage continued its calm descent.

He pounded on the call button. "Come on!" he implored. This he had to see again. "Come on, you sweet little bastard. Come back to Papa."

IN THE BASEMENT, Persephone went limp with relief the first time the elevator whirred. It could only mean Buster was in there.

As she pressed the call button, she wondered how he could have activated the mechanism. Maybe the tip of his horn had poked a button. The animal must have gotten the elevator to move somehow, that was all. No one else seemed to be loose in the house. She hoped. There hadn't been any cars in the driveway.

The elevator arrived, and Buster neighed a greeting as the grille peeled open.

"Bad boy, Buster," she scolded. "Don't you know elevators aren't for horses? What are you doing in there? Are you too scared to come out?"

Buster pranced restlessly. He didn't step forward.

Persephone sighed. "All right, I'll come in and get you. Somebody goofed when they gave you this drill bit you carry around on your forehead. It takes forever to get a headstall on you."

She worked at it, and finally the straps of the halter fit over his horn. Responding to her crooning tone, Buster leaned against her leg. Persephone kept a wary eye on the horn's tip. All of her jeans had fashionable holes from encounters with it.

"Okay, little guy, time to go back to your nice, comfy stable. What's—"

Persephone lurched, barely staying on her feet as the cage rattled and began to rise. Tripping over a small horse didn't help.

Steadying herself with a hand on the wall, she whispered, "This is impossible! Is somebody up there? Buster, what's going on?"

The cage went up a floor. Jarring to a stop, it settled with a noise familiar to her from a lifetime of rides. Dread magnified the sound to a crack of doom.

As the grille pleated open, her eyes met the gray ones of a grim-looking man standing in the main hall.

A tapering column of light spilled out from the elevator onto the hall floor. It caught the man full on. He seemed to be as flabbergasted as she was.

He was dark. Black hair, deep gray eyes, olive skin, black clothing.

But the light loved him. Blue-white highlights moved in his hair, though she was positive he hadn't budged an inch. A gleam lit the depths of his eyes.

His tanned face could have been molded from solid bronze, except it looked warm. Touchable. His black leather jacket fit his broad chest like a seal's gleaming pelt.

An eternity seemed to pass as she stood there, staring. But she knew perfectly well the door was calibrated to stay open only fifteen seconds. It clanged shut.

The noise jerked her out of the odd spell. She hit the down button, fast.

"Wait!" His voice was a deep rasp. An angry rasp. It fit him. "Hold on just a damn minute. I won't hurt you. I just want to talk—"

The elevator started down. He was only a few inches away on the other side of the grille. If she reached out her hand, she could have touched his fingers, which were clenched around pieces of the grillwork.

She didn't do it, of course. But the idea seemed natural to her. Weird, she thought. This was all weird, strange, wonderful. Real, but not quite real.

Like a dream. There weren't any rules in dreams.

The wide expanse of his chest appeared to float up as she rode down. At the last moment she looked up at his face. All she saw were his eyes. They bore into hers, gunmetal gray, but she couldn't read their expression.

Her mouth trembled into a smile.

The cage reached the basement. There certainly wasn't any rational reason to be happy—quite the opposite, in fact—but her smile wouldn't go away. It warmed her lips and gave her a melting feeling in her upper chest while she hustled Buster from the elevator and trotted him out of the house. It took some tugging. Finally she urged him out through her private door and into his lean-to.

"And stay here," she ordered, tying his halter firmly to a rail. "Don't even think about any more exploring, or—or you'll be sorry."

Buster sharpened his horn on the plank wall, completely unimpressed. They both knew she'd never bring herself to be severe with him.

HER SMILE CONTINUED to linger, as she ran around the castle and plunged into the concealment of a large pepper tree. The hanging branches and evergreen leaves provided a perfect hiding place, where she could see but not be seen. Leaning against the light brown trunk, she peered through the foliage towards the driveway. This was the likeliest exit for the man to take when he left the castle, unless—she shivered—he had entered the property along the same hidden path she had.

That worrisome thought made her smile fade. The dreamy feeling wore off. *It must be emotional overload*, she decided. A simple defense mechanism activated when she found Buster and herself under scrutiny. Persephone clutched her parka to her throat. What were she and the unicorn going to do?

And how much of the castle had the man explored? Desperately, she tried to recall if there were pictures of herself in any of the rooms. In a fury of grief and anger and disillusionment against her father five years ago, it had seemed very important to tear up every family photograph she could find and get rid of the pieces. Had she destroyed them all?

It was so long ago. Probably. But then, there was always a chance she had missed one. . . .

From her lookout point, she heard the crushed shell in the driveway give out a loud crunching noise. A car rolled to a stop only yards away. Persephone, who considered cars to be boxes on wheels at the best of times, couldn't identify the make. It was gray.

Like the man's eyes, she thought.

The sound of a car door slamming interrupted her thoughts. Beside the car stood another man, an older one judging from the bald spot imperfectly covered by strands of hair combed over it.

"Hey, Mack!"

She saw the dark-haired intruder let himself out the main entrance and lock it behind him. "Over here. Aren't we supposed to be the only ones looking at this property?"

"That was sure my impression."

Persephone closed her eyes. *Oh, no.* The stranger would go to the authorities and report a woman in the house. A woman with a unicorn.

She wished she could spit out some really terrible swear words. No doubt there would be plenty of opportunity to get used to swearing in prison. Probably her fellow criminals would share their expertise in self-expression while they all learned to make license plates together.

"You ready to go? Madeline asked me to remind you that you've got a meeting with your broker back in Portland. I've got your suit in the car."

"Right. Thanks."

The rasping voice didn't sound angry anymore, she noticed. Instead, it was intense. What would it be like to hear that voice under different, more personal circumstances?

In your dreams, she silently jeered. All you'll be hearing are jail doors clanging shut. And poor Buster—he'll be turned over to Leo, who'll turn him over to Chasmo.

She would do anything to keep that from happening.

But what, after all, could she do except keep on hiding? And where? Her thoughts went round and round uselessly.

Embarrassment heated her as he said, "I'll change here. Pass me the shirt and jacket. These pants'll do okay." He shrugged out of his leather jacket and the pullover sweater he wore underneath. His shoulders looked immense from this angle. They were the same warm bronze as his face and hands. "You're not going to believe what I saw in that castle, Joey."

Persephone knew she couldn't expect anyone to keep a story like this to himself. Dreading what he'd say next, she tensed.

"Wow," he exclaimed. "Hurry up with the shirt. It's cold."

"Cold as a witch's—er—mammary gland," agreed Joey.

"Why'd you say that?" asked the man named Mack, pausing as he pulled on the fresh shirt. An edge sharpened his question.

"Well—well, I don't know. Seemed appropriate. Must be this place. Right out of a fairy tale, isn't it?"

"Yeah." He finished putting on his shirt and suit jacket before taking the tie Joey handed him. "I think one of the resident sprites bewitched me. Or an enchanted princess, maybe. Yeah. An ice princess."

"Huh?"

"Somebody must have put a hallucinogen in my coffee this morning. Or maybe the old paint and wallpaper in there give off lead fumes. Can lead poisoning affect your brain?"

"I don't know. Madeline could call a doctor for you and ask. The library might be able to look it up. There's a poison hotline—"

Mack laughed. The rough, sexy chuckle seemed to go straight through Persephone. She shifted her position.

"Never mind," he said lightly. "You know how life can get sort of gray? Boring? And then—*wham*—something happens to brighten up your day? Seeing her—that did it for me. Even if she doesn't exist, I want to believe she does."

"Madeline?" Joey smoothed the long hairs over his bald spot. "Madeline's a great gal, Mack, but she's married. And she must have twenty years on you. Don't they have grandchildren?"

Mack slapped Joey on the back. Sounding amused, he said, "Not Madeline. My ice princess. She was tiny and exquisite and . . . all lit up. Platinum hair lying soft and windblown around her face and some kind of silvery thing for clothes." Persephone snuggled further into her parka of reflective material. He added, "You've never seen such blue eyes. Not pale blue like most eyes. This rare misty blue, like—"

"Sapphires? Topazes?" suggested Joey. He seemed to be catching the other man's mood.

"Nah. It's hard to describe. A blue like shadows under a frozen pond. If we'd stood and looked at each other any longer, I would have . . . hell. Forget it. The place got to me. I'm rambling."

Joey sounded shaken. "I don't know who this babe is, but boy, have you got it bad."

"Off balance, that's all. You should have seen what she keeps as a pet."

Persephone flushed. He'd mentioned her before Buster. Not everybody would find a pint-size blonde more noteworthy than a real, live unicorn.

"What's a woman doing in there, anyway?" asked Joey. "I'm *sure* you're the only prospective buyer the state people said they were giving a key to today. Aren't the grounds and house supposed to be locked up?"

He was a possible buyer? For *her* property? Maybe she'd better stop studying his muscles, she thought, and start resenting the heck out of him.

So far, the only good thing she knew about the man was that he didn't seem to know who she was.

"Seemed to me nobody else was supposed to be out here, too." Persephone didn't like Mack's thoughtful tone at all.

Then, with a shrug, he pushed his henchman into the car. "We'd better save our chitchat for the drive, Joey. I've got a meeting, remember?" A slam of his door cut short the final syllable.

Safer, safer by far for the sexy stranger to believe she and Buster were figments of his overheated imagination. Persephone waited for relief to wash through her. Instead, disappointment made her sigh and prop her chin on her hand.

Really masculine men normally tended to make her shy away. She didn't have confidence in her ability to control them. And Mack was the most blatantly virile man she'd ever seen.

It wasn't just his muscles. Brute strength didn't worry her. As a small person, she appreciated the value of brawn. A trifle uncomfortably, she admitted to herself that it—he, Mack—excited her sexually. But his voice, the way he held himself, the things he'd said, all proclaimed that he was a man who liked to be in charge. Five-feet-two of Persephone Snow couldn't possibly handle a man like that.

So why was she suffering from an urge to call him back? Especially when it would be better for Buster, and her, if he went away and stayed away?

She wondered what his last name was.

As the car made the wide swing around the driveway and headed toward the main gates, his face appeared in the rear window. Handsome or unhandsome?

Trying to view the man impartially, she peered at him. The features were rugged. That nose might have been broken some time or other; it had an assertive kink in the middle. The mouth was too hard and the jaw was carved out of granite.

Not handsome. But attractive. Any woman would respond to that rough-hewn strength. But his long, unsmiling stare at her childhood home scared her. Even after the car disappeared, she thought about that look.

The expression belonged to a determined man. One who, despite what he said, had no intention of forgetting he had seen a princess and her unicorn.

3

"WHAT ARE YOU DOING tonight?" Mack asked after his meeting broke up. Joey, who got a childlike thrill from driving his Lexus, had waited for him.

"Mack, you need to get out more," said Joey, stopping the car in front of the Quill and Grill, a hangout for Portland's local celebrities and members of the press. It was a saloon and steakhouse Mack had visited regularly at one time. Not lately, though. His ex-girlfriend was a reporter.

He was about to suggest they go somewhere else, when Joey said, "If you're looking for a good time, the one you ought to be asking out is your fairy princess."

Mack grinned ruefully. He did wish he could see the otherworldly blonde again.

"No time for fantasy dates," he replied, massaging the back of his neck. Tension had left knots right under the skin. "An afternoon listening to a broker pitch a stock offering leaves me more beat than a week at training camp. All I want is one quiet drink and then I'm hitting the sack—and the only thing I'm taking to bed with me is my laptop computer. I've got some figures to crunch on this shelter idea."

Joey shook his head. "Look, you're a young guy. In the prime of life. You got the money and the physique to have women drooling over you. Me, I'm an old guy. But not too old for love. I got a hot widow waiting for me with a meat loaf in the oven. *And* a fancy red nightie she puts on when we're both in the mood."

"Joey, I think I'm too young to be hearing this," said Mack, struggling not to laugh.

"I'm losing my hair, but I haven't lost anything else," Joey said with dignity. "Mack, a man has to find time for life before it passes him by."

"Yeah, well—"

"The way you acted over that blonde you saw—a man gets like that over a woman once in a lifetime. Don't let her get away. It'd be foolish to miss out on the real thing because you took a computer to bed."

The real thing. Had she been real? Bewitching was the word for the whole experience—the castle, the young woman and, especially, the unicorn.

The castle existed. But the other two? The unicorn had to be a normal animal doctored to look like a fairy-tale creature. Vaguely, he recalled hearing of a similar stunt. Hadn't a circus once displayed a goat with a single, surgically implanted horn?

But the blonde...Mack wasn't willing to dismiss the blonde as less than she had seemed. She had been alluring, enticing, and he wanted her to be flesh and blood.

A car horn blasted. Traffic clogged the streets at six o'clock on a Friday evening.

"I'll catch a cab home," Mack said quickly. What the hell. This was as good a place for a drink as anywhere else. He jumped out and then stuck his head back through the door for a last comment. "Enjoy the widow." Nudging the door closed, he stepped back as Joey joined the flow of vehicles.

Mack sprinted around a line of slow-moving cars. Double doors swung wide just as he got to the saloon. Into the dusk spilled light, voices and the smell of broiling meat.

"Mack!" exclaimed Bess Tallart.

Exactly the last person he wanted to see.

"It's been too long," she went on, smiling.

"Bess. I don't need to ask how you are. You look great."

Mack gave the compliment a careful just-friends casualness. A year ago, they'd been more than friends. Occasionally Bess showed signs of hoping they would become a couple again.

Although the reporter had been on her way out, she backed up, drawing Mack into the noisy saloon with a possessive hand on his sleeve. He turned to a row of pegs where a number of coats hung already. Sliding out of the leather jacket he'd thrown back on after his meeting gave him an excuse to shake off Bess's hand.

"So, how's life treating you?" Bess asked, unfazed.

"No complaints."

Bess made a face. "Can't you come up with anything more newsworthy than that? You're still a celebrity, Mack. Say something exciting and I'll quote you."

"You always did."

"It's my job."

She edged closer. One of her full breasts brushed against Mack's upper arm. He frowned. The seductive gesture had to be deliberate. Bess never did anything without a reason.

"I'm free tonight," she said, running a scarlet fingernail up his arm. "You look like you've knocked off for the day. We could go to my place."

"Uh, Bess—"

"You haven't forgotten how good we are together, have you? I haven't. God, Mack, I can't get you out of my mind. I'd even cook dinner, and you know I hate to cook."

The offer reminded Mack of Joey's widow. He smiled crookedly. Meat loaf in the kitchen and a fancy nightgown in the bedroom.

But Bess wasn't exactly the happy homemaker type. Ambition drove her dagger-sharp intelligence. Mack admired both qualities, along with her cool brunette good looks and her great legs. He was a man. If he let his attention dwell on those legs, and all the other nicely-put-together parts of Bess, he knew she could arouse him.

But he didn't want a cross-examination in bed.

"As I recall," he said, trying to take the sting out of his refusal, "you never cook without an ulterior motive."

She dropped his arm. "It still bugs you that I'm a reporter, doesn't it? Getting answers from people like you, people in the public eye, is part of my work. You resent it. You always did. That's why you broke off our relationship." The soft lighting from the bar didn't hide the rigid lines that sprang up around her mouth.

"Nah," said Mack gently. "I broke it off because, well, I couldn't shake a feeling that the answers were more important to you than anything else I provided when we were alone."

"You're wrong." Bess's boarding-school voice went low and hoarse. "So wrong, Mack. Come home with me, and I'll prove it to you." Her green eyes caressed him. The pink tip of her tongue touched her upper lip.

The mystery blonde had stared at him with eyes that threatened to consume him, too. Somehow that look was different from Bess's ravenous appraisal. A male wariness clicked on in Mack. Bess looked as if she were hungry and he was a steak sizzling on the grill.

"Sorry, Bess, I can't." Mack said it gently, aware of the people jostling around them.

"You mean you won't."

"We managed not to fight when we thrashed this thing out last year. Let's stay—"

"Pals. Of course." Her smile didn't erase the brackets of tension around her lips. "I'll buy you a drink. On the expense account. Apparently I can't talk you into a home-cooked meal, so the least you can do is let me interview you."

Mack didn't see any way out, so he shrugged good-naturedly and said, "A boilmaker."

She placed the order at the bar. They found a table. A waitress brought them their drinks, and Mack put a dollar bill on the tray.

"I would have taken care of the tip," Bess objected.

"I may know enough not to argue with a lady over the bar tab, but I can't get the hang of ducking out of the tip."

"What are you up to these days?" asked Bess, sipping Russian vodka.

"Just grabbing a quick drink and going on my way."

"Mack, darling, you've got to learn to push yourself forward. Get seen. Let me write a profile on you. You must be doing something interesting. People are always fascinated by sports figures."

He smiled easily. Handling the press was the same whether he was a boxer or a businessman. The trick was to act completely confident. Besides, he thought of a way Bess's desire to write about him could be turned to good use. A lot of people read the *Portland Voice*. An article about his plans to establish a shelter for homeless teens ought to garner some response. He needed to know how the public would react to the idea. It had already occurred to him that the smart thing to do at this point was to figure out the number of donations he could count on.

"I *have* got a project in mind."

Bess's sharp white teeth stripped lemon from the twist of peel that had come with her Stolie. "So talk."

"It's only in the planning stages," he warned. His whiskey had a satisfying bite. Mack followed it with a cooling sip of beer.

"A story, Mack. Come on. Human interest. Something spicy. Give."

Mack recognized the green glint in her eye. Despite her flattery, Bess would want more than a dull account of his attempt to start a shelter for street kids. Damn, after what he'd seen this afternoon, could he give her a story. . . .

He was still awestruck by what had happened at the castle. That bothered him. Awestruck wasn't a feeling he experienced very often. Putting the scene into words might shrink it into perspective.

He knocked back the rest of his whiskey. The heat it generated warmed him to the idea of opening up to Bess. "I've got a story for you. You're not going to believe it."

Bess promptly pulled a small tape recorder out of her purse and flipped the On switch. "Try me."

"I warn you, it's a real fairy tale."

Savoring his beer, Mack gave her the background. "You know what kind of neighborhood I grew up in. A lot of kids are still stuck in that cesspool...." He explained how he'd been looking for a large, vacant house outside the city to be used as a shelter. At the mention of the Snow castle, he could almost see her ears prick up.

Emphasizing that the property needed renovation to be turned into useful housing, he went over his visit— the overgrown grounds, the fully furnished castle empty of life, the elevator from another time moving by itself.

"All right, you've got me salivating," Bess admitted. "What happened next?"

A bustle next to their table interrupted them. She glanced up and annoyance crossed her face. "Firelli, beat it, will you?"

Mack recalled Michael Firelli as one of Bess's rivals on the *Voice*. A wiry man, he paused in the act of carrying a table to another part of the room.

"Hiya, Bess," he said. With exaggerated courtesy, he added, "Good evening, Mr. Lord."

"Firelli."

"What's the meaning of this intimate get-together? You lovebirds making up? Don't worry, Bess, I won't scoop you to the society column."

"Drop dead," said Bess.

"I'm cut to the quick. Well, lookie at this. A tape recorder. Hey, everybody, Tallart's getting an exclusive. Let's listen in."

Throwing the recorder into her purse, Bess snapped, "Firelli, I'll get you for this."

"Press conference time!" called Firelli.

"Pardon me. I'm getting another beer," said Mack.

He went to the bar for it, resigned to having a larger audience than he'd bargained for. Increasing by the second, a crowd of reporters followed him. By the time he'd blown the froth off a stein of foamy liquid, he was hemmed in.

Bess shouldn't mind the others hearing this part, he thought. He'd already given her the important, printable part of the story. The rest was just . . . reality that sounded like fantasy.

Leaning against the bar, he faced the throng. Bess was among them. She fit in. Like the rest of the reporters, she wore an attentive, calculating expression.

He swirled the amber liquid in his stein. There couldn't be any harm in sharing the story. It wasn't as if anyone would believe it.

"Like I told Bess, this is a fairy tale," he repeated.

"Cut to the chase, Mack!" called someone from the back of the crowd.

A slow, reminiscent smile spread over his face. "Today I saw a unicorn."

A belly laugh erupted. "A unicorn? Bess Tallart was recording a story about a unicorn?" Laughing helplessly, Michael Firelli clutched his sides.

Clown, thought Mack.

"Don't unicorns usually come equipped with maidens fair and all that crap?" Firelli chortled.

"Come to think of it," admitted Mack, "there was a young woman. She had the unicorn on a leash."

"A virgin?"

"Sorry, I didn't get to know her well enough to answer that question."

Most of the reporters were laughing now. One of them called out, "Well, was she at least hot-looking?"

"Hot?" The blonde, in some ways so icily perfect, had scorched him with those smoky blue eyes. That wasn't a detail he intended to share with these professional gossips. "Hot's not the right word. I thought she was cute. No, not cute. Beautiful."

Mack didn't realize how spellbound he sounded until the last word came out. Larynxes that suffered more than one throat punch developed rough-edged tones. But his voice definitely gentled when he talked about the blonde.

"Oh, God save us, a beautiful virgin and her unicorn! And Tallart thought there was a story in it!" Firelli just wouldn't shut up.

Mack's gaze happened to mesh with Bess's. Her mouth was tight and her green eyes blazing. Her fists clenched. She didn't look amused at Firelli's comments, either. But the anger clear in every indignant line of her body wasn't directed at her fellow reporter.

She was glaring at Mack.

THE BLONDE WAS all silver. White-silver hair floated loose around her face, blue-silver eyes smiled at him. Her gown of tissue-thin silver billowed in a warm breeze that stroked over her, and over Mack, like a whisper. It was a temptress's gown. The filmy stuff shifted over her breasts, her hips, hiding them one moment and revealing them the next.

Mack wanted her. Desire poured through him, clean and sharp. He felt powerful, hard, elementally male.

She walked toward him. Slowly. Seductively. The gown swirled out and then pressed close to her body, clinging. Her feet skimmed the grass. She came so close to him that the gown and nothing else, not even air, came between them.

Mack realized that he was naked in the magical moonlight.

Her silver arms went around his neck. The misty lights in her eyes told him she could feel the pressure of his arousal. Sexy as a single, chance encounter, innocent as a kitten, mysterious as woman, she rubbed herself against him. A deep breath shuddered through his lungs. Thank God, she wanted him, too.

"Take me now," she whispered. "Don't make me wait. Now."

Crushing the fabric out of the way, he braced his legs and lifted her. . . .

The burr of a phone ringing splintered the woman in his arms into fragments.

Mack struggled out of his dream, thrashing at covers that had wrapped themselves tightly around his legs. He picked up the clock radio from the table beside his bed. The glowing green numbers swam before his sleep-fogged eyes. It was 1:05 a.m.

The phone rang again, and Mack swore. Then he grabbed the receiver. "This had better be important," he snarled.

"Mack Lord? Knockout Machine Mack? Great, I caught you at home."

Whoever it was sounded cheery. Too damned cheery for 1:05 in the morning.

"Where else would I be? Like I said, this had better be important."

"I'm Vincent Arnsen, night editor at the *Portland Voice*. I'm calling to confirm a statement you made this evening concerning a, uh, a unicorn sighting. Can you confirm and would you care to comment?"

Mack swore again. "Are you crazy?"

"No, sir," the editor flashed back. "Are you?"

Rubbing his whiskery face with one hand, Mack jackknifed into a sitting position. His tired brain didn't want to think.

"I must be crazy to talk to a member of the press at this hour," he said wryly. "What have you got?"

"Just a couple of lines about a joke you told at the Quill and Grill tonight. All in fun. You know the kind of thing."

"Nothing about Ms. Tallert?" he asked, with the vague idea he'd have to ram his brain into gear and think fast if the item mentioned anything negative about his ex-girlfriend. That bastard Firelli might be using the incident to take a potshot at his rival in print. Although Mack didn't intend to get involved with her again, she didn't deserve to be humiliated.

"Bess Tallart wrote the copy," Arnsen replied.

"That's all right, then." Mack slid down into the covers and stretched out. Sleep beckoned.

"Mr. Lord? I still need a confirm or deny."

"Oh. Yeah, I told a story about a unicorn tonight."

"And a comment, please."

His chin made a rasping noise when Mack scratched it. "The story was clean, not X-rated, and it contained no slurs of any kind against unicorns. If the unicorn lobby wants to protest, they can do so tomorrow. Got that?"

"Got it."

"The real story is that there are kids living on the streets in this city who deserve a second chance in a safe environment. That's why I was out looking at the old Snow place. To see if it can be renovated for a shelter."

"Yes, sure. Thanks for the quote."

Mack put the phone down with a crash and flopped one arm over his eyes. The humorous part of the item was hardly news in his opinion. However, as long as Bess's embarrassment over the other reporters' laughter earlier in the evening wasn't made public, he didn't care if the paper put the unicorn on the front page. No one would take it seriously.

After all, he'd been careful to tell the absolute truth— just in a way that made it sound untrue. Everyone at the Q and G had laughed. The important thing, he thought drowsily, was that information about the shelter idea be included in the article.

The shelter wasn't what he wanted to think about right now. Maybe he could recapture his dream. The blonde had been so beautiful, so perfect, so willing.

He began to drift in a warm, sleepy darkness. *So willing...*

On the verge of sliding into unconsciousness, Mack felt the chill of an uneasy thought. He dropped his arm and his eyes slowly opened.

All the people in the bar had laughed. Except Bess.

THE NEXT MORNING, Persephone checked Buster's mineral salt, and then let him lick a handful of grain from her palm. His tongue was sandpaper-rough.

"Is that yummy? Better you than me, friend."

The rail was back in place, reinforced with extra nails. The feed box bristled with just the right amount of timothy hay. She was aware of his horn at the corner of her vision. Morning sun spun it into a spear of light.

"You're so special. I wish I could take you someplace where you could be appreciated by someone besides me. What's this thing made out of, anyway?" she said, running her fingers over the spiraling curves of the horn. Bone probably, she thought. That's what the vet at Ganders, Inc., had concluded. Nature had coated the mutated extension of Buster's skull with shiny enamel. "You're the prettiest genetic accident I've ever seen, that's for sure. And don't you know it!"

Leaving him to his breakfast, she decided that the morning felt right for a fast-paced hike around the property. Property that apparently no longer belonged to her.

And how do we feel about that? she asked herself, starting out on her walk. Not good. Most of her happy memories were tied up in this place. Vacationing with Grammy....taking long walks on the beach in search of seashells...sitting in her father's lap, imagining shapes no one else could see in the shifting fog.

There were not-so-happy memories, too. This was where the police had come to arrest her father. It was in the driveway that he'd had his heart attack.

So she'd gone away and stayed away. Only the necessity of hiding Buster had brought her back.

She glanced at the castle over her shoulder. It was big, gray and a horror to clean. And it was hers. Or at least it used to be.

There was nothing she could do about the tax sale now. She tried not to dwell on her sense of loss. If some sort of notification had been mailed to her old address, it must have been after she decamped with Buster. Going to a bank and mortgaging the castle to pay the back taxes was out of the question—no one must suspect where she was. While the specter of Leo hung over her, her whereabouts *had* to remain secret. All she could hope for was that the process of selling would take a while.

The best thing to do, she decided, was to sit tight, hide as well as she could, and see what transpired.

Yes, we're good at that. Persephone knew herself fairly well. *It's what we always do, isn't it? Hide when the going gets tough?*

She scuffed her pink high tops in the frost that covered the ground. On the weed tops, ice crystals sparkled like Christmas glitter.

Yesterday's sexy stranger hadn't seemed threatening, although he had appeared to be a lot of man. So much so that he continually made his presence known in her thoughts. She grinned with guilty pleasure—the kind of pleasure elicited by cream pie laced with rum or wearing silk lingerie on hot summer nights.

The fact remained that if he showed up at the castle again, she had to hide. Had to.

Persephone exhaled a long breath. Wistfully, she watched the feathery plume from her mouth swirl and disintegrate. *Had to.*

Reaching the border of the grounds, she turned back toward the castle. The frost crystals were melting, diamonds dissolving into tears. Without thinking, she cut across the old lawn. At the castle she glanced back, and saw that she'd left a trail of trodden plants behind her. Bending, she lifted a saucer-shaped milkweed flower and then let it go. It flopped.

Shrugging, she turned to the lean-to. Sturdy, intertwining plants shielded Buster's home. They appeared to hug the outer wall. Bottlebrushes and wisterias tangled together in a seemingly impenetrable lattice of branches and gnarled vines.

Inside it, Buster whickered.

"Do you hear me, sweetie?" asked Persephone, finding the narrow tunnel she'd carved in the vegetation. She passed through. Plopping herself down in a clean corner of the natural clearing where she'd built the lean-to, she let him curl into her lap.

"You don't have to worry," she murmured, hoping she was telling the truth. "Persephone will keep you safe. But you know what? If I'm going to spend a lot of time daydreaming about Mack, it would have been nice to know his last name."

MACK WOKE AFTER a restless night almost as groggy and bad-tempered as he'd been when Arnsen had called him.

Naked, he did a few leg lifts and back stretches to wake himself up. Then he tugged on sweats, went to the door of his ultramodern house, and picked up the morning paper. Breakfast, he was thinking. Something unhealthy and loaded with cholesterol. Bacon and eggs. Hash browns. Industrial-strength coffee.

He put breakfast together and sat down with the *Voice*. His brainstorm had made page one of the editorial section.

Reality Check, Mack?

Beauty has her beast, and modern-day princesses claim they date frogs more often than princes.

This tradition of human contact with the non-human world continued yesterday, when Knockout Machine Mack Lord met his first unicorn.

Lord, former heavyweight champion undefeated in thirty-five fights, described the close encounter of the strange kind to an audience of appreciative reporters at a popular nightspot. With his pet project to start a shelter for runaway teenagers in the works, the inevitable question is, "Would *you* trust your charitable donation to a guy who sees unicorns?"

"Damn," he said.

4

MACK STOOD AT THE FRONT door of the Snow castle and jingled the keys in his pocket. In one arm he held a deli bag. At his feet a bedroll leaned against a small grip containing his shaving kit and a change of clothes. A laptop computer, battery-powered lantern, portable CD player and small TV, as well as a thermos and a box of bakery goods, littered the flagstones.

The pastries were for tomorrow morning. He was hoping by the time breakfast rolled around, he wouldn't be eating the apple Danish alone.

Right now it was late and dark. Invisible in the shadows, his car stood in the driveway. The sound of the sea was a far-off pounding. As he knew from his drive along the coast highway, there was fog lurking offshore, but it hadn't crept to land yet. A sliver of moon formed a Cheshire cat grin high in the black sky. Stars sparkled with extra brilliance in the clean air. Their glitter was cold, though. As was the temperature. The castle was a grim, looming presence.

At ten o'clock at night, the estate retained its fairy tale feeling. But it was the atmosphere of the old, grim Germanic tales, not the happy Disney versions. The place oozed an offbeat charm. However, it was impossible to ignore the odd sense that beings not quite human held their revels here.

He whistled tunelessly through his teeth. Tonight the atmosphere didn't bother him. After all, he'd been through hell this week already. The national media had picked up the *Voice* story; he'd even been featured on an entertainment news show.

Mack wasn't angry about the snickers. He'd opened his own big mouth and given Bess the opportunity to make a fool of him—and God knew it wasn't the first time he'd been foolish over a woman. There wasn't a man alive who hadn't, at one time or another.

And you're doing it again, he thought. Only partly was he here because of the unflattering news reports. Of course, it would be nice to catch the unicorn and show it off, show that he wasn't a punchy ex-boxer whose brains, if he'd ever had any, had been beaten out of his skull long ago. Mack had a sense of humor, but it stopped short of enjoying being a laughingstock.

It was crystal clear that nobody was going to make donations to fix up a shelter founded by a madman.

The setback drew out Mack's strong streak of stubbornness. He would buy the damned castle and he would produce the unicorn. Donations would flood in to remodel the place. The shelter would be a success. Period.

But he was also at the Snows' front door in the cold, star-splattered night because this was where he'd seen the blonde.

Despite the fact that he was thirty-two, relatively intelligent and hardly the romantic type, he had this need, this ache, to meet her again. Life for him had always been ruled by clocks and objectives. Too ruled by them, maybe. Unfortunately, his break from an active career hadn't satisfied him, either. His existence had leveled into a holding pattern. The idea for the shelter was the first thing that had excited him in a long time. But it hadn't put any light into the flat, boring gray that oppressed his, well, his soul. Only the blonde had done that.

Even a tough guy who'd worked his way up from grimy gyms needed a little magic every now and then.

A flashlight stuck out of his jacket pocket. Mack fingered the long smooth handle, then pulled it out and switched it on. Its beam played over the door. Turning, because it always made sense to check his back, he ran the light over the field behind him.

"Bingo," he said, pleased.

A path that hadn't been there a couple of days ago cut through the tall weeds in a nice, straight line. Somebody had been on the property. It could have been a meter reader. Just as easily, it might have been kids from Rockaway or Wheeler, looking for a thrill, a quiet place to pop a six-pack or some privacy to defy their elders' warnings about premarital sex.

Or it could have been the blonde.

Thoughtfully, Mack slid the keys out of his pants pocket and let himself in. Marble rang under his feet. The temperature was the same as it had been the first time he'd been in the hall, pleasantly cool but not cold. Compared to the outside air, it felt warm. He turned on the chandelier and started to set up his minicamp.

He'd be hard to miss. That was his purpose. He intended to make himself very hard for the blonde to ignore.

Unrolling the sleeping bag, he placed the lantern nearby and flicked it on. Then he turned out the overheads. No point in advertising his presence to anyone outside the castle. The location, high stone fence and encircling plants made it unlikely casual observers would notice light leaking from the narrow windows. Still, he didn't want to take the chance. This was personal.

He sat cross-legged on the sleeping bag and shucked off his shoes. His black jacket and shirt followed the leather mocs. He nearly always slept nude. Under the circumstances, however, Mack decided to keep on his jeans. His princess *had* looked virginal—as if he were the first man she'd ever seen, in fact—and he didn't want to shock her.

Damn, but he would feel like a fool if she didn't show....

There was a Natalie Cole album in the CD player. He hit the On button, and Natalie's creamy voice filled the room, picking up ghostly echoes in the corners of the vaulted ceiling.

He bet the song was flowing down the elevator shaft like glitter swirling in a glass snowball.

"That'll lure her out," he told himself in satisfaction.

THE MUSIC CAME from everywhere and nowhere.

Persephone sat bolt upright in bed. Violins and sax, and a female voice. The walls vibrated with melody.

She could feel the sting of air as her eyes opened wide with delight. Delight was idiotic, because something very out of the ordinary had to be going on, and that couldn't be good news for her and Buster. There were people in the house. There was music. But, oh, it was lovely to hear the old place come to life.

Persephone, she thought, *you're finally flipping out. Find out what's going on before you go all gooey and sentimental.*

Getting out of bed, she slid her feet into thick socks and tugged jeans on under the long, white T-shirt she wore instead of a nightgown or pajamas. Her hair bristled with static. She gave it a halfhearted push off her forehead. It could be Leo up there. The likelihood of Leo mixing business with violins seemed small, but . . . There were a lot of things she could be arrested for. It would be hideously embarrassing to go to jail looking like this.

She didn't have much choice. Somebody had to go upstairs and find out where the music was coming from. No one else seemed to be volunteering.

The socks muffled the sound of her feet as she ran lightly through the daylight basement to one of the secondary staircases. She went up carefully; they were uncarpeted and slick, and it was dark.

The stairs ended in the large upstairs kitchen. Although she couldn't hear music anymore, she was an insulated distance from many parts of the house. The tune might still be playing. So Persephone went on quietly, feeling her way as she went forward into a corridor that led to the front of the castle. Gentle piano chords began to drift from the hall.

A husky voice sang about honesty and fear and the stages of love. Dan Hill's "Sometimes When We Touch." It had always been one of her favorite oldies.

Another man's voice, even lower and rougher, joined in. She stopped just short of a corner, her heart slamming in slow, painful strokes. The second voice was familiar. It rambled along with the tune for a few lines, then dropped into a hum.

Why him? she thought, biting her lip. At least it wasn't Leo, but what was the sexy-eyed stranger doing here?

At least the situation didn't seem to be leading to an arrest . . . unless the stranger normally serenaded wrongdoers before he busted them. That didn't seem too likely.

Persephone decided there was no point in being a martyr and denying herself a glimpse of the man. Perhaps he'd turn out to be—she didn't know—smaller, wimpier, less male than her memory of him. She hoped. One peek, she vowed, and she would melt back into the shadows.

Scooting cautiously around the corner, she risked a quick look. Her heart went into overdrive. She forgot about merging with the darkness. Instead, she stood stock-still with the blood pounding in her ears, and stared.

How could a man's body be so beautiful?

He was sprawled half in and half out of a wide black sleeping bag. Instead of a pillow, a soft-sided piece of luggage supported his thick, sloping shoulders. A lantern's round eye cast a beam on the computer screen in his lap. The light reflected off his craggy face and intent eyes, and created shadows that defined the muscles of his chest. Those shadows moved intriguingly as his fingers danced across the keyboard. All the parts of him not swathed in sleeping bag were bare.

Until now, it had been easy—all too easy—to visualize him as masculine . . . but not handsome. His face was all planes, as if hacked by an artist determined to chisel elemental strength. But even if "handsome" wasn't a word anyone would apply to his features, the rest of him was gorgeous. Those pecs alone would cause strong women to swoon. No doubt the guy had a multitude of options for lovers.

Too male, too smart, too apt to be distracted by other women. Definitely not the kind of hero she would ever choose.

Not that you're looking for a hero, she told herself severely. *You're not a brainless, clinging, passive princess too wussy to figure out your own escape route from an enchanted castle.*

She took a silent step backward.

"I don't bite," he said, not looking up from the monitor. "Unless I'm asked to, of course."

Smooth, pal, Mack thought. Real smooth. After that clumsy start, the best he'd be able to do was convince her he was a diamond in the rough. Which was true.

Reaching out rapidly, he turned the lantern so its light streamed toward the hint of white that had alerted him to her presence.

She lifted a hand, palm out, to guard her eyes.

"Sorry," he apologized, and adjusted the lantern so it wouldn't shine directly in her face. "Don't run away again."

Her hand fell. She looked young and defenseless in the softer light. The loose white garment she wore could have been an angel's robe from a Christmas card.

"You'd just chase me, I bet." Her statement sounded more breathless than bitter.

"Yeah. I probably would." With a stab of a finger, he cut off the music. Taut silence stretched between them. "Like some crackers and cheese?"

A smothered sound reached him. It might have been a startled giggle. "What?"

"I brought some deli stuff. Drinks, too. Do you prefer mineral water, beer or wine cooler?"

She flattened herself against the wall. "It's a little late for me."

Mack flipped the cap off a beer bottle and sipped. The tangy liquid trickled down his throat, reassuringly normal. His laptop made little be-bop computer noises as he exited from the list of figures he was working on, and then the sounds cut off mid-hum when he shut the machine down. He pushed it off his lap.

"The cheese is good." He broke off a piece and popped it into his mouth.

"Has it occurred to you that camping out in a deserted castle eating cheese is, you know, kind of strange?" she asked tactfully.

"Oh, yeah. Definitely." He shrugged. "Don't you ever act on a whim?"

The question won him a tiny smile. "All too often."

She had small, regular features, saved from chilly perfection by a stubborn and fascinating mouth. The full upper lip peaked sharply in the middle, where the dip was drawn in a deep, sulky line. Her lower lip looked kissably soft.

Mack was watching the lower lip when she added, "You don't strike me as being a quixotic guy."

"Good. I think."

Her lips stretched into a brief, enchanting curve. "'Quixotic' means foolish and impractical. Rash. Romantic."

"God, no." He held out a cracker topped by cheese striped with orange rind.

"You're trying to tempt me."

"Is it working?" Her blue eyes studied the cheese yearningly, but she didn't answer. He continued, "Look, I don't blame you for being wary. You'd be insane not to be. Unless there's someone else squatting in this place, you're alone with a strange man in a very big, very empty castle. All I can say is I'm not here to hurt you. And I don't intend to roust you out so you end up on the beach."

She shoved platinum hair out of her eyes in an indecisive gesture. Then, slowly, she edged closer until she could drop down next to the sleeping bag.

"That floor's hard and cold," Mack pointed out. Shifting his bottom, he made room for her on top of the sleeping bag. "Have a seat."

Expressions played across her face. Shyness, doubt, a feminine embarrassment he couldn't fathom. "Oh, all right," she said crossly, and crawled onto the quilted material. Gracefully, she curled her legs under her, sitting with her back extremely straight. The message was clear. *I don't quite trust you.*

"Here." He put the tidbit to her mouth.

It opened in what looked like an automatic response and he slid the loaded cracker in. Her lips nipped his fingers softly in closing. For a moment, neither of them breathed. Then he withdrew his hand. She chewed down on the morsel of food with a sudden crunch. Her eyes were big and startled.

"There's something I've been meaning to ask you," she said once she swallowed.

"Have you?" A warm, pleased feeling spread through him. She'd been thinking about him. He hadn't been obsessing alone. "What is it?"

"I know you're thinking about buying the castle—"

"More than just thinking. I am going to buy it."

Indignation flashed in her eyes. The pleasant warmth faded.

Coolly, she went on, "I don't know anything else about you. Like your whole name."

That wasn't so bad. "Mack Lord. The Mack's short for MacAdam. It was my mother's maiden name. My parents hoped her rich brother would put me through school or leave me his money, or something. He didn't." Mack waited, but she just nodded in understanding and reached for another piece of cheese. "What's your name?"

Instead of eating, she broke the cheese into smaller and smaller bits. "Penny. Short for—Penny."

"No last name?"

"Nope."

He watched her begin to nibble her Havarti crumbs. "Any particular reason you're hiding out in this pile of rocks?"

She froze with a palmful of cheese lumps halfway to her mouth. "Hiding out? That's quite an assumption, isn't it? Why can't I just be a tourist attracted by a castle?"

"Hearst Castle is a two-day drive down the coast. It's open to the public. This castle isn't." Mack sighed. Alienating the blonde wasn't part of his plan, but it had to be said. "You're trespassing. And you're living here— unless you usually go around admiring old buildings in the middle of the night, wearing your woolly socks and nightshirt. Besides, you're forgetting one thing, Penny."

"Am I?" she murmured. Her pink tongue came out to lick the cheese from her palm, and Mack almost groaned aloud.

"Yeah," he said roughly. "Where are you keeping your unicorn?"

5

"MY UNICORN?"

The face she turned to his was sweet and innocent. Mack's experience didn't include a lot of sweet and innocent.

But he did believe Penny had never discovered the alluring magic of her own sexuality, had perhaps never even been with a man. Not because she looked so much like a virgin. But because otherwise she'd be trying to vamp him, he thought cynically. She wouldn't have to vamp very hard, either. His flesh already ached. The sense of wanting must have shown in his expression, because she flushed and dropped her gaze.

She cleared her throat delicately. "Most people don't put much faith in unicorns, Mack."

"They haven't seen one. I have."

"Um, it's getting close to Halloween. Maybe you saw a dog or something in a costume."

"What I saw looked an awful lot like a golden retriever with an ice cream cone glued upside down on its head. But it was a horse," he said impatiently. "A horse with a horn. Last time I heard, that's a unicorn."

"Sounds like it," she agreed judiciously. "Did anyone else see it?"

"Only one beautiful blonde who seems to have developed a memory lapse."

Shakily, she said, "Oh, well, you know how blondes are. Not too bright."

His hand gently crushed a strand of the fair hair that fell to her shoulders. "I don't judge by stereotypes. What about you? You strike me as an intelligent person. Isn't Penny smart?"

"Going by Penny's behavior right this minute, I'd have to say no."

Her breathing was quick and shallow. Under the loose nightshirt, her small, round breasts rose and fell. He watched them. The wanting sharpened, concentrating in his lower body.

She objected, "Mack, don't. You promised no physical stuff."

The silky hair clung to his fingers. It was thick and soft. Her verbal gymnastics were a clear indicator he wasn't going to get any answers about the bizarre animal, anyway. Mack decided he might as well say what he'd come to the Snow castle to say.

"Correction. I said I wouldn't hurt you. There's nothing on the table about seduction. Can you be seduced?"

She sucked in a small, shocked breath. "You don't believe in beating around the bush, do you?"

"Waste of time."

"Time," she said, as if she'd been inspired. "You can't seriously be suggesting that we, uh, do anything when we've known each other twenty minutes!"

Shaking his head, Mack replied, "Half a week. I figure we've been acquainted at least seventy-two hours. I've thought about you. Dreamed about you, even. Seeing you in the elevator—it was a lot like getting clobbered across the face with a two-by-four. I felt stunned. I still do." He let a few heartbeats pass. "If you don't know what I'm talking about, then I guess I am wasting my time."

Abruptly, she pulled her hair from his touch. The locks slipped through his fingers. Uncurling her legs, she rearranged them so she was sitting tailor-fashion, and propped her elbows on her knees. With a shiver, she crossed her arms. The pose, which he sensed was unconscious, transformed her from a virginal angel into a pixie pondering a problem.

"Maybe I do know what you mean," she admitted, not looking at him. "It doesn't follow that anything's going to happen. I can have impulses and never act on them.

He couldn't decide if she was saying she was attracted to him—or just the opposite.

Nothing ventured, nothing gained. "My sleeping bag's a double," he pointed out.

Her arms crossed tighter. "You're going too fast for me, Mack. Even if it's been more than twenty minutes, we haven't exactly been getting to know each other. And a few days isn't that long. Men and women don't jump into a sleeping bag together after—I mean—" Her eyes finally met his. He could feel a grin plastered all over his face. Uncertainly, she finished, "They don't, do they?"

"It's been known to happen, Penny."

There was no longer any doubt about it in Mack's mind; she *was* a virgin. Oddly enough, the urgency of his need faded into a background ache. It didn't go away, but the level of painful pleasure became tolerable.

The emotion that overshadowed male need startled him—it was male protectiveness.

Somehow he'd actually found an untouched maiden right out of a fairy tale. Damn. Virginity was hardly an issue to him; as far as he knew, he'd never been a woman's first, and it had never been a matter of regret or relief. But this particular virgin appeared about as able to defend herself from the big, bad modern world as a mythical princess.

Not at all.

Did she have a job? Hell, she didn't even have a home if she was living in the castle.

"You've never been in anybody's sleeping bag, have you?" he asked, beating down the compulsion to touch more than her hair. "Never had any experience."

"Getting kind of personal, aren't you, Mack?" Persephone shifted again, pulling her knees up under her chin and wrapping her arms around her legs.

A flush covered her whole body. She could feel it.

Her breasts absolutely, positively, noway could be swelling—breasts couldn't do that. Furthermore, it was years since she'd reluctantly come to the conclusion they had grown as big as they intended. But with Mack's hard gray eyes all over her, the small, sensitive mounds felt heavy in a way they didn't usually. She was aware of them pressing against her T-shirt.

Hot, moist sensations quivered between her legs. And the muscles in her legs were melting to the consistency of warm taffy.

Heavens, she thought, he hasn't even touched me. What'll it do to me if he does?

"How old are you?" he demanded.

"Twenty-two," she retorted, staying in her defensive ball. "How about you?"

"Let's just say about the time the baby doctor was swatting your cute bottom to get you to cry, I was pasting one on Ricky Ruiz. We were ten. It was my first knockout punch."

"You knocked another child unconscious?" Persephone could hear the note of disapproval in her own voice. She inspected the muscles in his chest and arms again. Mack must be as strong as he looked.

Why did she have to be a sucker for muscles?

"I was more surprised than Ricky was. In fact, I was scared spitless I'd killed him," he said, leaning back on his makeshift pillow. His eyes glinted reassuringly. "Hell, Ricky was my best friend. Happily he came to right away. I picked him up and dusted him off and let him give me a black eye. It all came out even. We're still friends, as a matter of fact."

"If you say so." She tried to imagine little girls staying friends under those circumstances, but couldn't. "Men are different from women." Wrong subject, Persephone thought. She retreated to the former topic. "Uh, so why were you fighting?"

The reminiscent sparkle in his eyes darkened to a flat gray. "He made some comment about how poor my mom and I were."

At her questioning glance, he shrugged his big shoulders.

"Ricky was right. We weren't dirt-poor, but close to it. My pop was a factory worker. He was killed in an industrial accident. No insurance. Mom worked her tail off, but her job as a hairdresser barely kept food on the table."

Persephone didn't know what to say. There was nothing self-pitying in Mack's remark; if anything, he was matter-of-fact.

"Sounds like a hard childhood," she offered.

"No worse than a lot of kids'. Better than some. I always knew my parents loved me. That's the important thing to kids. The worst was getting over the feeling Pop had abandoned us by dying. Nobody likes being left." He paused. "I don't know why I'm telling you this."

Persephone didn't know, either. But the instant soul-to-soul communication felt right. "Maybe because it's late and dark outside and we're all alone."

He put down his beer. "Maybe. Anyway, I got lucky when I was fifteen and landed a job in the local gym, as a sparring partner. I caught a boxing promoter's eye and made a nice living for a while."

"Just a nice living?" she asked shrewdly.

He grinned. "I didn't want to boast. It was a *real* nice living. Mom wouldn't leave the old neighborhood, but I bought her a livable condo and, well, she'll never have to stand on her feet all day again."

"I'm glad."

"In some ways, you might say I've lived a charmed life. Escaped from poverty, got into and out of boxing with no major injuries, had a pleasant life-style the last few years. No money worries."

"That must be nice," she said—wistfully, he thought. So the blonde was broke? Of course she must be. Why else would she be living here? "And now you're interested in buying a castle," she added.

"Yeah. I got out of northeast Portland, but a lot of kids live on the street there. It's too easy for the girls, especially, to fall into drug use and prostitution."

Persephone didn't know what to say. That her father had been an expert on the subject? She contented herself by nodding.

"This place could be a shelter for them," he went on.

She looked around. "A shelter?"

"It would need a little work," he said defensively.

"I'll say."

Pectoral muscles popped into impressive relief when he tucked his hands behind his neck. There was almost no hair on his chest; the skin was smooth and sleek. Under his arms dark curls clustered. Somehow the contrast emphasized his masculinity.

"You don't read newspapers or watch TV much, do you?"

"Not lately," she admitted. "What have I missed?"

"Nothing important." Persephone could feel him studying her. "So tell me about Penny," he said.

It was the name an eight-year-old Persephone had wished her parents had given her. She couldn't tell him that. Hunching her shoulders, she lowered her gaze to the floor.

"I take it we're not going to talk about you?" he asked. When she glanced up, she saw his hard mouth quirking at the corners.

She bit her lip, not answering.

"Well," he continued after a thoughtful moment, "you think it's too soon for sex, which would certainly be *my* choice—"

Persephone wondered if it was possible to die from a blush.

"—And I've been talking too much, and about the damnedest things. If we're not going to hear all about your life, what's next? How about a cozy chat about the unicorn?"

She shook her head.

"Then we can eat some more," he suggested. "Or listen to music—I've got Cole, Hill, Air Supply, Clint Black. We could make like an old married couple and watch TV—"

She interrupted him. "Morning comes around early. I'm going to bed."

"Not alone." His growled objection halted her halfway to her feet. "A gentleman always walks a lady to her door."

"That's not necessary," she protested, straightening.

"You mean you don't want me to find out where in this relic you've set up *your* camp."

He sounded amiable, or as amiable as his harsh, throaty voice could. Still, Persephone watched him warily. He dragged himself from the sleeping bag. She suppressed a gasp. His jeans in no way hid his masculinity. They might as well have been leotards, or not there at all, because the clinging black denim completely failed to mask the tightness of his buttocks and the long, heavy muscles in his thighs.

"Really," she repeated, dragging her gaze away, "it's not necessary for you to walk me anywhere."

His rough-hewn features arranged themselves in an expression of hurt. "Don't you recognize a gentleman when you see one? The evening may have been short on candlelight and romance, but give me credit. I did my best. Classy music, fancy food and, hey, I offered you a beer."

She struggled with laughter. "What more could a woman ask?"

"Right."

The way his eyes crinkled at the corners when he smiled demoralized her as much as his scratchy, intimate voice and frankly male body. This man wasn't just sexy, he was dangerously likable.

That was curious, since they had nothing in common. She shouldn't be drawn to Mack at all. They came from different backgrounds. She'd dreamed of a strong but sensitive hero. Somebody who'd do what she told him to do while being unfailingly polite—polite enough, for example, to pretend he'd never seen her unicorn. Instead, she'd gotten a Prince Charming who barged into her affairs completely uninvited. A hard-eyed man who exuded a take-charge attitude.

But she was attracted. Very attracted.

And he seemed to enjoy her company, too.

Grabbing a flashlight, he sprang up in a lithe motion. His actual height only grazed six feet. However, since she stood exactly five feet two and a half inches, he towered over her.

"Let's go," he said, still pleasant and still implacable.

"I don't have to show you where I sleep."

"Fine. Which half of the sleeping bag do you want? I usually take the left side, but I'm willing to make an exception."

Shoving her bangs out of the way, she spun on her heel and stalked to the crooked stairs that led to the daylight basement.

"This place is a rabbit warren," he commented, shining the flashlight down the narrow cavity.

"Us rabbits like it."

Her socks gave almost no traction on the varnished wood. To save herself from slipping, Persephone clung to the banister as she descended.

The stairs ended in the servants' kitchen.

He passed the flashlight over the room as they entered. Since she forced herself to be fanatical about cleanups, there was no sign of her simple evening meal. Counters were bare, their delft blue surfaces all wiped to sparkling innocence. The very lack of dust must look suspicious, she thought with an inward groan. Mack stopped and opened the refrigerator. Her yogurt and cold cuts sat in lonely isolation on the top rack.

Beneath them stood a series of coffee cans. He raised his brows. The light bathing his face from the refrigerator's low-wattage bulb made him look stern and pale, like a judge.

Uneasily, Persephone said, "I guess that seems like a lot of coffee cans."

His thoughtful noise didn't reassure her. Pulling out a can, he nudged the plastic top off and stared inside.

"It's not drugs or something, if that's what you're thinking," she added sharply.

Mack realized he was looking at horse feed of some kind. But he decided if she wanted to play it as if there were no horse, he could play it that way, too. "I don't know what to expect from you," he replied, straight-faced. "But it sure wasn't—dried corn?"

She shrugged.

The other cans revealed more corn, the cracked kind, as well as oats, protein meal, wheat bran and dry molasses.

"This junk must make one hell of a gritty granola," he said finally. "You *eat* it?"

Hoping to get away with as few lies as possible, Persephone replaced the containers and slammed the refrigerator door. "I keep everything in the fridge because the cold and dryness cut down on mold."

"Okay."

She glanced at him suspiciously, but he seemed prepared to take Buster's rations at face value.

He picked up the flashlight. "Are you a health food fan?"

She wasn't, but given Mack's mistaken conclusion she could hardly say so. "Health is good. It beats being sick. Don't you agree?"

"Sure. Oh, speaking of health issues, in case you were wondering, I don't sleep around. In fact, there hasn't been anybody for a while. Whenever there was, I was always careful."

His directness flustered Persephone. Mack was honest. Up-front about his motives, crystal clear about what he wanted.

He wanted . . . Penny. The mystery girl in the castle. The one who didn't exist.

In reality there was only Persephone Snow, with the oddball name and the oddball little horse—and a heap of problems.

Resting her hip against a counter, she tried to give an impression of blithe unconcern. "I think we should avoid getting too personal, Mack."

"Then one of us has a problem." Turning the light on her, he spoke out of the darkness. "I feel very personal toward you."

There were long, safe inches between their bodies. Somehow Persephone felt surrounded, outmatched. Nearly seduced.

Without speaking again, she spun around and almost ran out of the kitchen. Her beeline led into a corridor lined with doors. Behind them were a pantry, laundry room, wine cellar and a series of small suites for the former live-in staff. At the end of the hall, almost unnoticeable in the shadow of a freestanding wardrobe, came the last door. Her door.

Pausing, she glanced back. Mack was right behind her.

"This is it," she announced defiantly. "I sleep here. You are not coming in, so don't even think about it."

"No wonder I didn't find your hideout when I went through the castle before." Mack surveyed the setup. "You sure you're not going to run away during the night?"

"I'll be here in the morning, okay?" She waited for him to leave. He didn't. She demanded, "Is there something else?"

"Mmmm?" He crossed his arms. The beam from the flashlight in his hand veered wildly. "I was just thinking about ways to seduce you."

"How you can talk about . . ."

When her protest petered out, his lips twitched. He went on in a reasonable tone, "You seem man-shy. I guess the most effective thing I can do is give you some space to make up your mind about me."

"Fine!" she said, recovering her voice. "Give me lots of space."

"You've got it. For a while."

How long was a while? Persephone had a horrible thought. "Has the castle already been sold? To you?"

"I've got my bid in. It'll take a little time before the state closes the bidding. I expect to win."

She just bet he did. He didn't look like the sort of man used to losing.

But at least the property hadn't changed hands. Yet. For some reason, that gave her a feeling of security. The castle might not belong to her anymore, but it didn't belong to anyone else, either.

Mack ambled toward the stairs.

"Wait a sec." Peeling off her socks, she tossed them to him. "The floors are like ice."

He pulled them on. The tops barely reached his heels. "Thanks."

"And conserving water is really important to me. Would you mind not . . . flushing . . . unless it's absolutely necessary?"

"I'll try to remember that," he said gravely. "Good night, Penny."

He got as far as the entrance to the corridor before he glanced over his shoulder. The glow from the flashlight barely reached her.

"You know, if you're running away from something—or somebody—I might be able to give you a hand. I've got some business connections. My friends might be able to get faster action from the police than—"

"No police," she said quickly.

"Is it the police you're running from?" How was he able to make his voice so soft and beguiling?

She tried to stare him down. Though it was hard to make out his features behind the flashlight, she doubted she was succeeding.

"Penny's not your real name, is it?"

She stood her ground. "Go away, Mack."

"Not till you give me some answers. Ones that make sense. But for now—good night, princess."

6

LOOPING A PLASTIC TIE around a garbage bag, Persephone said, "We've got problems, Buster."

The horse snorted.

"Really," she insisted, heaving the bag up and over her shoulder. She wrinkled her nose at the pungent odors escaping from the tightened hole at the top. "He's not awake yet, but how do I act when he is? I mean, who would have thought the man would actually spend the whole night? I half expected him to be gone this morning, but I took a peek and, no, he's still there, snoozing away."

He'd been lying on his side with one bare shoulder visible and his head pillowed on his soft luggage. Mack Lord had looked like a man who'd settled in for a nice, long stay.

She snapped the railing closed. "Perhaps he'll get tired of sleeping on the floor," she said without much hope. "I can't let him see you again. Do you realize if he does, he'll have to turn us in or become an accessory to grand theft? We have to keep the dratted man from ending up in that position."

It had been easy to picture herself allowing the nonexistent hero of her imagination to risk felony charges along with her. But she couldn't do that to Mack. Why, she didn't know. She just couldn't.

Buster didn't have a reply. His velvet nose snuffled in the new straw she laid to replace what was in the garbage bag. Persephone smiled at him affectionately. "I know, you want to play. We'll have a workout later. I promise."

Trudging to the woods, she dumped the contents of the bag under bare-twigged bushes. Good, natural fertilizer, she assured herself. A glance confirmed that Buster had no digestive problems or parasites.

As soon as she buried the empty, reeking bag under loose dirt and leaves, it was a relief to stop by the van for a quick cleanup with the baby wipes she kept under the front seat. The smell she brought with her into the basement a few minutes later might be antiseptic but at least it was un-horsey.

Pale sunshine flooded through the short, wide kitchen windows set high in one wall. During her brief absence, Mack had obviously woken up. Despite the earliness of the hour, he was dressed in shirt, tie and slacks. He was bent over a white cardboard box.

"Honestly, Mack. Stuff from the bakery? It's not good for you." She tried to sound as if the contents of the box didn't smell heavenly.

"I know. That's why I like it." The freshly shaven face he turned to her was easygoing. His slow hi-there smile did funny things to her insides. "But you don't have to eat any Danish. I mixed you a bowl of your granola."

Her gaze switched to a bowl she recognized as one of a set from the cupboard. It was filled to the rim with . . . Buster's feed.

Mack returned her panicky look with one of pleased expectation. Obviously, she was going to have to eat it. He handed her a spoon. She crunched her way through a spoonful. How did Buster chew all the gritty pieces? She was lucky not to crack a tooth. Swallowing heroically, she put down the spoon. "It's great. Thank you."

He glanced at the still-full bowl. "You're welcome." His innocent expression didn't falter by so much as the flicker of a dark eyelash. "Sure you wouldn't like a Danish, as well? I can't eat all of them."

"Well, if they'll just go stale..." Persephone was proud of the dignity she managed to give the objection. Unfortunately, the impression was ruined by the speed with which she snatched a pastry.

"I don't mind sharing."

With her mouth full of meltingly soft pastry and the flavors of butter and spice, she thought about his marvelous early-morning voice. A rusty, no-apologies-about-being-male voice. It sent a rasp of female appreciation along her nerve endings.

Reaching for a roll, Mack said, "You'd share your granola if I wanted some, right?"

"Definitely," she said feelingly. "Have all you like."

"That's what I thought."

The satisfaction in his reply roused her suspicions. Her eyes narrowed.

"Want to talk about your unicorn yet?" he asked, confirming her guess that he knew the "granola" was horse feed.

"Nice Danish."

Grinning, he agreed. The rebuff didn't seem to bother him. The man was armor-plated in self-confidence. She wondered what it would be like to feel like that. She never had.

No, that was wrong. Under ordinary circumstances, she dealt with life just fine. Persephone had talents and good qualities, and she recognized them. The problem was her confidence as far as men were concerned. It had gotten ripped out of her when she was seventeen and had discovered the man she loved most in the world wasn't what she thought.

He sheared off about a third of the roll. A dot of amber jelly squirted onto the inside of his index finger. Unembarrassed, he chewed and swallowed, and then lifted his hand to lick it off. The tip of his tongue showed between his lips.

With far too much vividness, Persephone could imagine the heat and moisture of his tongue, the hard warmth of his lips. Sweet jelly, salty skin.

Her breakfast plopped to the counter in a shower of icing flakes. Mack glanced from the Danish to her face, and slowly straightened.

He intended to be patient. Incredibly patient. Unthreatening. Last night he'd barely touched her before both of them retired to separate sleeping quarters. His questions had created an uncomfortable feeling between them, it was true. But he'd been careful not to pressure her in any way—not even about her animal companion. The only temptation he was flaunting at the wary blonde was sin for breakfast. Even that was innocuous. Sugar, not sex.

Apparently, his good intentions were paying off already. Her eyes had softened with desire to a cloudy blue. A flush rode high on her cheeks. He almost groaned aloud when he looked at her mouth. It was soft, vulnerable. Pink. Moist. Slightly open.

Slowly, afraid to spook her, he stretched out his hand.

"Apple," he said.

Persephone hesitated. The tragedy of having zero self-esteem when it came to really masculine men was that a woman never opened herself up to the fun of flirtation. The opportunity was here. The opportunity was Mack. All she needed was the confidence to take a chance. On him. On herself.

So delicately he had to concentrate to feel the contact, her lips closed on his finger. So soft. Unbelievably soft.

"Kiss me." The hoarse demand was out before he knew he was going to make it.

Without replying in words, she released his finger and lifted her face. Her mouth was free; Mack took it.

He whispered a kiss across her lips. Nothing hard, no demands. Just a gentle courting, the barest sensation. She tasted sweet.

She kissed as if it were the very first time. Only their mouths touched, but he could sense her body going still and rapt. Her lips didn't move, and yet they... accepted...him. They surrendered, drawing him down into a well of velvet darkness. His mouth brushed lightly, tenderly. He gave in to the experience.

Whatever her background, Mack was definitely no virgin. Kisses, and more, had been part of his dealings with women since he was fourteen. But this was different. Who would have thought he could ever feel as if his soul were being wrenched straight to the surface of his body, where she could touch it?

He wasn't used to the feeling of union. A shudder ran through him and the strange impression of souls naked to each other wore off. Or maybe it just settled deep inside him.

She was still there, her lips warm, moist, soft in unconditional surrender.

Mack shifted impatiently. His body wanted more. His soul wanted more.

She looked at him and smiled. "That was nice."

"Just nice?"

"Better than nice."

He kissed her again, deeply this time. He wasn't sure what he expected. To discover the secrets of her mouth, certainly—where she liked to be cherished and how her body would react if he rubbed or sucked or nibbled. The discoveries came quickly, because his mouth roamed hers like wildfire. At the first pressure against her upper lip, she sighed luxuriously and tilted her face up to his. A thorough exploration of her lower lip dragged a tiny noise from her throat. One of her hands clutched at his shirt. When his tongue swept back and forth between the sensitive corners, she closed the inches between their bodies with a gasp.

"You don't kiss fair," she whispered into his mouth.

"Me?" He trailed a long kiss from her cheek to her ear. It was a very pretty ear, hidden under flossy hair. He teased the lobe with his tongue. "Who started this?"

"Don't expect complete and total honesty while you're . . . um . . . driving coherent thought out of my head," she complained.

The arm that was free slipped around her waist, anchoring her against his swift hardening. Mack couldn't quite believe this was happening. Couldn't trust his senses to verify that they were doing this. The setup— castle, girl, unicorn—was illogical. Magical. Part of

him wouldn't have been surprised if she behaved like
an ice princess in a fairy tale and melted like snow in his
arms.

His grip tightened. "Are you real?"

"I've never felt more real in my life." Her palm mas-
saged the dress shirt covering his chest, as if she were
trying to get used to the feel of a man.

"I don't suppose you'd like to tell me what you're doing, living in a vacant building with that crazy animal."

Mistake. All her supple pliancy stiffened into a defensive, starched-up stillness. Then, carefully, she
peeled her hands away from his chest. Stepping back,
she picked up the roll and took a bite.

It seemed to be an effort; she chewed slowly and
swallowed while blinking against a shine of tears.

Frustration dug claws into him. "Caring enough to
ask questions makes me the bad guy, huh?"

He turned and fumbled with the thermos. In the act
of pouring coffee into cups he dragged from a cupboard, his hand jerked. Too much unexpended energy.
His nervous system was clanging like a fire bell...from
a few kisses.

To distract himself from the persistent ache in his
groin, he looked around vaguely for some way to clean
up the spilled coffee.

She was ahead of him, wiping the brown liquid with
vigorous strokes of a paper towel.

"You're a fanatic about clean, aren't you?" he said at
random.

"Not really." She balled the towel in a small fist. "But
we both know I'm not supposed to be here. It's only
common sense to cover my tracks as well as possible."

"Penny..."

Mack's curiosity rode a teeter-totter with caution. *She sounds genuinely bitter.* Then he realized that a better description was scared out of her tree. Her rosy flush had died away. Pale, her skin formed a revealing background for the bluish smudges under her eyes. Tension tightened the little muscles of her face. Her eyes were stubbornly free of tears, but the blue had gone dark with confusion or indecision.

He ought to push it. Get as many answers from her as he could while she was vulnerable and might let something slip. She'd trusted him for a few minutes, in his arms.

It was that short-lived trust that changed his mind. He couldn't bully her. Not after the kind of kiss they'd just exchanged. He couldn't resist the lost look in her eyes.

Wanting her seemed to be as natural as breathing. But sometime in the last four tumultuous days, had he fallen not only into lust, but into love? With "Penny"? A woman who didn't even trust him with her real name?

Ridiculous.

This was a hell of a time even to think about it. His schedule today included a breakfast meeting with an architect to discuss remodeling the castle, and lunch with a team of professional fund-raisers. His mail needed to be picked up. And Joey would be expecting him at the gym.

A workout was a damned good idea. He had a lot of frustration to work off.

He would rather stay here—not because he wanted to concentrate on his search for her unicorn. No, the main attraction as far as he was concerned was the woman nervously shredding the damp paper towel in her hands to bits.

Feeling pressured, he checked his watch. Hell, nearly seven o'clock. It was an hour and a half's drive to Portland, which would make him only slightly late for his first meeting. In the meantime, he couldn't leave her with her hands so nervous she was a menace to inanimate objects.

"Listen," he said rapidly, "I'm worried about you. If you're involved in a scam—"

"What?" The look of anxiety disappeared into one of sheer surprise.

"There has to be a reason you're hiding a unicorn," he rapped out. "But your pet isn't my main concern. You are. Isn't there anyplace else for you to go?"

"No."

God, she was homeless.

"Family?" he probed.

"'Fraid not. My mother died before I can remember, and my father—is dead, too. So are all my grandparents. No aunts, uncles or cousins. I don't have a job, either, so my options are limited." Her chin came up proudly.

"There are agencies that can help." He tried to say it gently. "Shelters and low-income housing. If you've somehow avoided learning any skills . . ."

"I don't have any I can use."

He noted the careful phrasing, but didn't know what to make of it. "Then you ought to be in school, getting some. I can find you part-time work. . . ."

Crisply, she said, "No thanks. It so happens I'm not an object of charity yet. Maybe you don't approve of how I'm getting by. That's just tough, Mack."

He felt helpless and didn't like it. Why couldn't he reach a happy medium with women? There'd been Bess, who always wanted something from him. And now there was "Penny," who wouldn't take anything he could give.

With another glance at his watch, he scowled and took her by the shoulders. "Don't freeze me out, ice princess. We've just started to make some progress."

Before she could duck, he kissed her. It was quick and hard. An "I'm going now but don't forget where we left off" statement on his part. Even so, when he lifted his head, his breath was ragged and "Penny" . . . her eyes were still closed and her lips slightly parted.

Reluctantly, he released her. "I have to go," he said roughly.

She opened her eyes, slowly, dreamily. As her gaze lingered on his expression, a frown pinched the smooth skin between her brows. "Are you angry?"

"Yeah. I've got dragons to slay in the real world."

A pause lasted long enough to become awkward. He wondered if she was hoping he would say, *But I'd rather be with you.* Mack clenched his jaws against the words.

When push came to shove, no matter what had transpired between them, he and she were strangers. Probably incompatible strangers at that. She was all spun-silver magic. He was battered and rough-spoken and used to fighting his way out of tricky situations, in the ring or on the stock market or in the media.

Persephone held her breath. If he said, *I'd rather be with you,* she might cave in to the impulse to tell him everything. All her secrets, including Buster, would come tumbling out at once.

A muscle tensed along his bluntly carved jaw.

When the silence stretched itself past the breaking point, she let the air out of her lungs. "What kind of dragons?" she asked, pouring the cold coffee down the sink and rinsing the mugs under a thin stream from the faucet.

His smile bent wryly at the corners. "Turn on the morning news and you'll probably find out. I've got to run. By the way, you're not getting rid of me. See you tonight."

His leaving left a vacuum. Persephone told herself firmly that the house was no more empty than usual.

Suddenly starving, she picked up the remains of her roll. With a hand under her chin to catch crumbs, she bit into it and wandered up to the main floor. Mack's portable TV squatted among his other things in the middle of the hall. She clicked it on. By some accident of atmospherics, the set homed in a clear picture.

The news was just beginning. Curled up on his rumpled sleeping bag, she sat through disasters and commercials. Despite the roll, her body felt hollow. It's not food you want, she told her appetite. That's just a substitute. Be honest, you want Mack.

The desire was sharp and specific. His bedding gave off a slight male smell that didn't ease it one bit.

Man-hungry. She turned the phrase over in her mind. It didn't sound very nice. She'd known she was ready for a relationship, but that was different. Being biologically fine-tuned in theory wasn't as scary and wonderful as the wallop packed in Mack's kisses.

Her body wanted Mack's body. Worse, although she wanted Mack in a way that included sex, the totality of her feelings surpassed sex by a country mile. If he had pressed her, she would have made love with him on the kitchen counter . . . and what she would have been offering was far more than a willing body.

You can't fall in love with him. You just can't.

Buster was a compelling reason to keep her emotional distance. With one eye on the screen, she pulled up her knees and rested her chin on them. Even if Buster had never existed, she and Mack were an impossible combination. The last thing a man like Mack—a good man, who went around helping kids—needed was a felon for a girlfriend. Especially a felon named Snow. He'd made his feelings about her father's line of business plain last night.

Now the repressed memories stirred.

SHE'D BEEN FULL OF DREAMS once, before the bottom fell out of her privileged life. Mainly young Persephone had dreamed about Johnny. With his lean body poised above a surfboard, he'd made her the envy of the beach every time they drove down to Malibu. That was the only place in California to surf—according to Johnny. Odd how she'd never realized what a snob he was.

Or perhaps it wasn't so odd. How many seventeen-year-old girls would see past his blond good looks? His big-man-on-campus popularity also had blinded her. He was captain of the debating team *and* varsity quarterback. Best of all, Johnny pulled back when she protested taking things too far and too fast in the back seat of his sports car. She had wanted him to respect her. It thrilled her when he said he did.

The younger Persephone never suspected that Johnny's interest in her was low—so low that he didn't consider her worth the bother of talking into sex. Only two kinds of women existed to an ambitious young man like

Johnny. The kind you slept with, and the kind you were seen with.

She was an ornament as far as he was concerned. Like the best car, or the correct clothes. A trophy girlfriend. After all, she was the picture-perfect daughter of financier Thomason Snow.

When Thomason's arrest ended in the intensive care room, Johnny went with her to the hospital. He held her hand while she cried, looking through the glass at the tubes and wires attached to her dying father.

Then, still holding her hand, he explained that she couldn't be his girlfriend anymore. "We're young," he told her earnestly. "The ink on our high-school diplomas is hardly dry. You'll forget me."

"I won't," Persephone contradicted him. She blinked back tears. The scales were falling from her eyes. "Believe me, I'll never forget this."

Johnny took her words at face value. "Listen, I've already got my life mapped out. The right college, the right law school. Perhaps someday a seat on the Supreme Court. It's not out of the question for somebody like me."

"You mean a bright, handsome young man with great family connections?"

He'd shrugged modestly.

"And of course you can't jeopardize your glittering future by hanging around the daughter of a criminal."

It had been a quick cure for naïveté. And a valuable lesson.

FINALLY, PERSEPHONE thought, she was at the point where she no longer associated sex with the mockery of love sold by her father, or with the sting of rejection

inflicted by Johnny. Mack had thrust himself into her
life. Mack, who *was* interested in her. Whose plans
definitely included sex.

But not so long ago, Johnny had judged her unfit to
be the woman for a man in the public eye. What had
changed, really? Nothing.

The news droned on. Finally, toward the end of the
broadcast where human interest or humorous stories
were usually placed, a newsreader chirped, "And here's
the latest on embattled boxer-turned-businessman
Mack Lord...."

Persephone stopped morosely licking the last few
flakes of icing from her fingers and listened.

Snippets of news footage flashed on the screen behind the reporter—Mack in boxing shorts, landing
punches reinforced by huge gloves; Mack shaking
hands with community leaders; Mack stirring a caul-
dron of beans at a soup kitchen.

"Popular with fight fans for his punishing left and
with Portland's northeast side for his devotion to good
causes in that troubled neighborhood, Mack Lord is
being dogged by a joke that went sour. Knockout Machine Mack's tale of meeting a unicorn has catapulted
him back into the glare of national attention—but
there's no sign he's happy to be there."

In the next clips, Mack gave increasingly brief re-
plies to reporters who crowded closer and closer with
notebooks and microphones. Persephone gulped. He'd
told. About Buster. In public, apparently.

What a mess. No wonder he kept asking about the
unicorn. How could she possibly prove to everyone
that Mack wasn't crazy and protect Buster at the same
time?

Those reporters were like vultures picking over a tasty carcass—except that Mack wasn't dead. Yet. One of them, chasing him up some steps, was so beautiful that Persephone breathed, "Wow." The woman was tall, the way she'd always wanted to be tall. Exotically brunette, the reporter had eyes of so striking a green they showed up as vivid emerald on the small set.

The way those gem-colored eyes tracked Mack's athletic figure . . . cold fingers seemed to walk up Persephone's spine. Whoever the reporter was, there was personal feeling in that glance. Intense, inimical personal feeling.

Persephone poked the Off button with more energy than necessary. Untangling her feet, she stood up.

First things first. If Mack was coming back tonight, then she'd better make darned sure the castle was swept clean of any photographs of her. She was almost positive there were none, but better better safe than sorry.

An oil portrait of herself in a smocked dress and flowered hat wasn't dangerously recognizable, she decided, standing in the first-story parlor that had always been used as a living room. In fact, the portrait barely resembled her at all. The Persephone on canvas was only nine years old, and the artist had painted her face as a childish blur. Huge eyes and shadowy features.

The castle really was big. An appreciation for its size hit her as she trudged from room to room. Too big for one person. She thought of the housekeeper, two weekly cleaning women and gardener who had once worked here. Her amused humph echoed. Just keeping the basement kitchen and her own quarters tidy wore out her patience.

Her step started to lag as she headed toward the elevator. Stepping into the cage, she reluctantly activated the machinery. The other rooms that needed checking were bedrooms. Hers. Grammy's. Her father's.

Grammy's room was empty of any photographs except for a sepia-tinted picture taken at least sixty years before. Arathea's shingled hair went nicely with Grandpa Snow's rigid collar. They posed next to one of the horses Grammy loved, and they looked young and breathtakingly happy.

Persephone smiled mistily and said, "Hi, Grammy. Hi, Grandpa." This was a photo she hadn't been able to destroy—and she couldn't do it now. At least it wouldn't lead Mack to guess she was related to any Snows; both of her grandparents had square faces and prominent features.

A cursory glance at her own old bedroom showed no remaining photographic evidence of her life. The bed, too, was missing; she'd dismantled it and brought it to the daylight basement. Without its main piece of furniture, the room seemed strange. Rather sad.

On impulse, she opened the closet and peeked inside. Outdated clothes hung in a neat row. A croquet set and some paperbacks were scattered across the floor.

Ready to close the closet again, she glimpsed a hint of pink. Her old "dress-up" dress! It was actually a nightgown of Grammy's—fifties vintage, she guessed from its style—and how she'd loved it as a child. In it, she'd been Cinderella at the ball, Sleeping Beauty startled awake by love's first kiss. The gleaming folds reminded her of a time when she still believed that dreams could come true. She hadn't experienced such a sense of wonder for years . . . until Mack had kissed her this morning.

The pink satin was in amazingly good condition. Suddenly impatient with nostalgia, she swept the nightgown off its hanger. Who knew, maybe the gown would fit. It would be fun to wear satin to bed some night.

Holding the nightgown in her arms, she left her room and went to one down the hall. With a toe, she nudged open the door.

One quick look verified that there were no pictures on bureau drawers or bedside tables. She'd done a thorough job, five years ago.

As swiftly as she looked, she had the door to her father's room closed again. It was only a closed door. Not the person who used to live behind it. But she found herself saying, "Why did you do it, Daddy? Did you think I wouldn't love you if there wasn't any money? You were wrong."

The door didn't answer.

Up here, it was impossible to forget she was his daughter. The child of a man no better than a pimp . . . who was trying to hide her past from a man who despised the world's oldest profession.

Clutching the pink nightgown to her chest as if it were a talisman, she ran for the elevator.

Her new bedroom, the one she'd furnished for herself in the basement, looked reassuringly familiar when she dropped the gown off. Everything was all right. Everything would stay all right. Time might fly, but enough of it remained to plan the next escape she'd have to make with Buster.

Only this time, they'd be running away from Mack. From kisses that filled her with dreams again.

She went outside. Even a fresh, blustery wind didn't do much to blow away her feeling of being hunted by her own thoughts. Letting herself into Buster's stall, she automatically ducked away from his horn and patted his neck.

"Time for some dressage practice. You could be a champion at the horse shows—if you fit into a category." Confining her thoughts to the present, she reached for the straight twig she used to signal his paces. "You know, boy, I said we had problems. I didn't know Mack had them, too. Let's think about it. There must be something we could do to help."

IN THE STUFFY AIR of his motor home outside Los Angeles, Leo Ganders patted his forehead with a handkerchief. "Yes, Mr. Chasmo. I understand the problems of your filming schedule."

The phone squawked.

"Of course, Buster's in perfect health. No, why would I be stalling on the delivery? There are just a few details to take care of, I swear. Like what? Uh, Buster's mother. She's suffering from what-do-you-call-it. Separation anxiety. We had to call in an animal psychologist. The shrink says it's a bad time to take Buster away from her."

The phone squawked again.

"Soon, Mr. Chasmo. Soon. I promise."

Hanging up thankfully, Leo breathed a sigh. Not a sigh of relief. A sigh of rage.

It was getting harder and harder to soothe Chasmo's suspicions that something had gone wrong. All he needed was time. Nobody knew better than he did how hard it was to keep a sensation like Buster secret. Eventually, a certain blond do-gooding bitch would be found out. And when she was, he'd be ready.

Shaking open his newspaper, he scanned the front page.

Slowly, he smiled.

7

"Hi."

Persephone glanced up at the greeting. "You shouldn't have come back."

He rolled his shoulders in a tired shrug. "I'm just not a liberated kind of guy. I don't like the idea of you spending nights alone in a spooky place like this."

"I can take care of myself. The castle doesn't scare me."

"Well, it gives me the willies. You can protect me."

She gave in to the impulse to smile. "My hero."

Not so long ago—the day she'd kidnapped Buster, in fact—she'd wished for a hero. Mack, who was obviously as stubborn as a mule, wasn't precisely what she'd had in mind. Possibly she'd set her sights too low. He was a lot better than what she'd imagined she needed. It was just her bad luck that if she threw herself at him and revealed all, she'd make him a party to her crime.

Under the circumstances, calling him her hero struck her as unforgivable the moment the words left her mouth. Okay, she'd kissed him this morning. But a woman with felony grand theft charges hanging over her head shouldn't flirt as if she were welcoming a lover. Especially when the man was in no way, shape or form attached to her.

"If the castle makes you think of things that go bump in the night, why do you want it for a shelter?" she asked in a strained voice.

"Because the ghosts will get tossed out on their fannies when it's remodeled," he replied briefly.

The wind had died down, but goose bumps stood up on her arms. She was one of the ghosts. "Go on."

"God, what a day. Lunch left a bad taste in my mouth. I spent the afternoon punishing myself in the gym." Mack glanced from a rosebush to the clippers in her hand. "Getting in a little pruning?"

"Just cutting out the worst of the deadwood. It's the wrong season for real pruning. I don't know why I felt like doing it today."

That was another lie. She knew very well what had prompted her to attack the brittle canes in the formal garden. There was nothing she or the horse could do to help Mack without endangering Buster. Nothing. It was a bitter pill that wouldn't wash down. Still feeling frustrated after the session with the unicorn, she'd hunted up clippers in an unlocked garden shed, and put in physical labor on something that would at least show the results of her effort.

He nodded approvingly at her tall pile of thorny branches. "You got a lot done."

"Not enough." The autumn garden spread out around them, its stunted or sprawling plants a testament to neglect. Tendrils of fog snaked in from the ocean. Misty jaws gradually swallowed trees and bushes. "The place looks like it's under an evil spell, doesn't it?"

"Not all spells are bad." His eyes were weary, but they smiled at her.

Was he recalling their morning kisses? She certainly was.

A rush of remembered passion warmed her fingers and toes, and spots in between. The October air might not be freezing, but it wasn't tropically hot, either. Nevertheless, Persephone pulled off suddenly sweltering gardening gloves. For good measure, she loosened a button on her blouse.

Casting around for something to say, she stammered, "Um, it's the cocktail hour. Would you like me to get you one of the beers from the fridge? After all, they belong to you."

"I feel like a change. Let's go out."

"Out?" she asked, horrified. Leaving Buster, now that he'd discovered he could break out of his pen, was a terrible idea. And encouraging Mack was worse.

"Yeah. You know. Out to dinner. I know you like to eat."

She let the teasing remark pass. "I'm not in the mood for a restaurant." Actually, dining out sounded like heaven. Trying for a light note that wouldn't reveal too much, she went on, "You could pick up some takeout and bring it back here."

"It's supper time. I want soup. I want a thick salmon steak and dessert."

"I could make you a salad," she offered.

"Out of what? Oatmeal, or whatever your canned junk is? Thanks but no thanks."

Her list of objections was running thin. Salmon. Moist and silky and filling. Lightly brushed with butter and basil. "I'm not dressed to go out."

He surveyed her pink overalls and the cherry red shirt she wore underneath. "I like the way you look," he said.

"But if you're worried, the restaurants in Rockaway are what you might politely call casual. They don't care what you're wearing as long as your pockets are lined with cash. That is, my pockets. I'm paying and no back talk."

"I can't let you—"

"It's a business dinner," he said unexpectedly. "When it's business, the employer has an obligation to pay for the employee's meal."

"You're not my employer!" For the first time in the discussion, Persephone felt on safe ground. She balled her hands on her hips.

"Yeah, well, I intend to talk that over with you."

"Not Rockaway," she said suddenly.

"What?"

Feeling foolish, she explained, "I don't want to eat in Rockaway." Too many people might recognize the little Snow girl, all grown-up. Wheeler had the same drawback. The only place worse than the beach towns would be Portland. Once upon a time, her family had been socially prominent in the city.

"Then let's make it Tillamook. I can think of a place where the food is good and everybody wears jeans. Does that sound acceptable?"

" . . . Okay."

Feeling outmaneuvered, she let him take her gloves. He paused, studied the dirt-encrusted canvas, and then shrugged, flicked open the briefcase in his hand and tossed them inside. Persephone winced, thinking of garden soil and thorn tips streaking his papers. But if he didn't care, she couldn't see why she should.

He drove the gray box she'd seen before. Inside it was unexpectedly comfortable. She sank into buttery leather and breathed the intrinsically masculine scents of a fine car—cowhide and polished wood and the faint bite of gasoline and motor oil. It was a far cry from her ancient van. Comparing this to her transportation was like comparing a brand-new skyscraper to prehistoric rubble.

"I'm going to get dirt on your seat," she warned as he yanked on his seat belt.

"It'll brush off."

Even if Mack didn't treat his car like a love object, Persephone couldn't relax.

Her jitters stayed with her even when he turned in a modest circle and headed down the driveway at a reasonable speed. Thank goodness. Apparently Mack wasn't one of those guys who roared around proving his manhood by how dangerously he drove.

"I like you, Mack." The admission slipped out.

He touched her hair fleetingly. "I like you, too."

Reaching the big double gates at the end of the driveway, he put the transmission in park and glanced at her. "I'll get the gates. Jump over the gearshift and take the car to the road. I can close up behind you."

Obeying, she steered carefully, stopped the car outside the gates, and squirmed into the passenger seat again.

As soon as he rejoined her, she asked, "What was that for? To see if I can drive, or to see if I'd steal your car?"

"Neither." His laugh was like pebbles rubbing together. The sound eased her jumpy nerves. "All I wanted was to get the gates shut." He paused. "Is that why you're hiding? Did you steal something?" He put it together too fast. "Princess, does the freak pony belong to somebody else?"

Every muscle she owned tensed. "I'll make you a deal. You act like we're out on a regular date and I will, too."

It wasn't much of a deal, as she was well aware, but he nodded with brisk pleasure, as if she'd just offered the moon, with diamonds and rubies thrown in. "Sounds good. Don't forget, though. I want to talk some business with you, as well."

True to his word, he took her to an unpretentious steak and seafood restaurant. Persephone was happy to note casual clothes on most of the patrons. Her overalls fit in. And the food was ambrosia. Despite the impression given by neon beer signs flashing pastel colors over paper tablecloths, the sourdough bread was crusty and the salmon broiled to tender perfection.

"This is great," she said sincerely as the waitress left them to strawberry cheesecake, "but I'm not sure it's business."

"Yeah, it is," he corrected her. "I'm about to offer you a job."

"Mack, I told you, I'm not trained for anything I can work in right now."

"This kind of job doesn't require a degree." Digging into his cheesecake, he smiled at her.

An intuition hit her, and she carefully laid her loaded fork onto her plate. "No degree, no experience."

"Right."

"And I'd be working just for you."

"Right again."

A lump the size of Mount Hood filled her throat. How could she have been so wrong about Mack? Evidently he wasn't averse to a little sex-for-pay at all. Well, Thomason Snow's daughter was.

"Is there something about me that makes you think I'd agree to that sort of—arrangement?" she demanded.

Leaning back in the booth, he raised his dark brows. "Only the fact you seem to be broke."

"Broke doesn't make me desperate, mister. And I'd have to be a whole dimension beyond desperate to prostitute myself."

There was a deadly, loaded silence.

"What the *hell* do you think I'm asking you to do?"

His reaction confused her. "I thought—I wouldn't— maybe I jumped to the wrong conclusion. Let's try again. What is this job?"

"Going through my backlog of mail."

"Oh." She spoke in a little voice. Appropriate, she thought, since she'd rarely felt so small in her life.

"Want to explain that conclusion you jumped to?" Mack's tone made his question an order.

"Not really."

"Do it anyway." Reaching over the table, he took her chin between one big thumb and one big forefinger.

She looked everywhere but at him. "A lot of guys expect dates to pay for dinner afterward. *You* know."

"With sex."

"With sex."

"And you've decided I'm one of those guys."

If she hadn't found courage from somewhere— maybe from his level tone—she wouldn't have glanced up and caught the flash of hurt in his steady gaze. But she did. Oh, Mack, she thought, do I have the power to hurt you?

The realization made her feel even more wretched. "Maybe I was scared you would believe *I* was the kind of person who thinks of a date as a mercantile trans-action. I tend to be hypersensitive on the subject."

"Any particular reason?"

My father ran a prostitution ring. She drank iced water, and swallowed the words.

"Call me eccentric," she said at last.

"Like a little old lady?" Through his grip on her chin, she could feel the anger run out of him. He snorted. "Nah, I wouldn't call you eccentric. Although you're certainly one of a kind." His fingers turned gentle and slid down her throat before he let her go. "So do you want to hear more about the job or not?"

Did she? Persephone wasn't sure. She fidgeted, wishing she could avoid the issue. The decent thing would be to get him out of her life, not to go along with a plan that would bring them closer together.

She didn't know what to say...and she couldn't seem to stay still. Her napkin fell to the floor; she leaned sideways and picked it up. The dessert plates needed to be stacked; she stacked them. When there was nothing useful left to do, she did useless tasks. Mack simply watched her. Catching his gaze on her fingers as she lined up dirty forks, Persephone ordered her hands to fold themselves, tidily, on the table. Pride demanded at least a pretense of serenity.

Quietly, she said, "Thank you, Mack, I'd like to hear about the job."

AS THEY LEFT the restaurant, the marquee of a movie house blinked at them from across the street.

"Come on," said Mack abruptly. "You need a break from thinking so hard. Let's take in a movie. Something that doesn't require us to do anything except sit there with our eyes open."

His hand enveloped her smaller one like a big, warm glove. He jaywalked her to the ticket box. Persephone considered hanging back, but a glimpse of his face changed her mind. The gray eyes were hooded, his mouth was a slash above a jaw hacked out of granite.

Mack didn't look like a man who could be argued with.

He bought her more stale popcorn drenched in butter-flavored oil than she could possibly eat. The seats he nudged her toward were in the center of the front row.

"You have to sit up close to appreciate a really bad movie," he lectured, sprawling in his seat and stretching out his legs. He scooped up a handful of her popcorn and fed it to her kernel by kernel. The blunt tips of his fingers brushed her lips. The salty flavor burst on her tongue.

"Why are we going to the movies?" she asked when her mouth recovered from the assault of sensations. It tingled. "What is this film, anyway?"

"We're sitting in the dark eating popcorn to get you to relax. Who knows what the movie's called?" He glanced casually at the still-white screen. "It'll be bombs going off and guys shooting each other and finally the world gets saved but only after most of it has been blown up. A typical Chasmo production."

The bucket of popcorn tipped off her lap to the floor.

SHE SMILED STIFFLY. "Good night."

Not budging from her door, Mack jiggled the flashlight thoughtfully. "Are you mad at me?"

"Of course not." Persephone shifted the heavy load of mail from one arm to the other. "Why should I be?"

"Search me. But you obviously hated the movie. And you've said about three words in half an hour which, frankly, isn't like you."

"Are you saying I talk too much?" she asked sweetly.

He opened his mouth. Then he closed it. She could almost see him counting to ten. "I'm saying you're driving me nuts. And wild. So what's new? Good night, princess."

Safely barricaded behind her door, Persephone couldn't throw off her mood. She *had* been stiff and silent. Her defensive sulk had begun at the restaurant, continued through the movie, and persisted during the drive home. In the strained quiet of the car, she had fantasized about doing something to break the tension—grabbing him and kissing him, or picking another fight with him, or even bursting into tears. He was so darned perfect. And she couldn't have him.

It took only a minute to sneak out her door and check on Buster. Cosy in his stable, he was sleeping. Persephone blew him a silent kiss and came quietly back in.

Riffling through the letters he'd given her from his briefcase, she decided to stay up and get a head start on her new job. The decision to attack the stack of correspondence was easy; she felt charged to the topmost hair on her head. As if electricity had replaced blood in her veins.

She chose a piece of lined paper covered with a penciled scrawl, and read it through. Then another. And another. Time eased past while she read steadily. Every once in a while she groaned. The people who wrote

Mack didn't seem to have access to typewriters or computers—or dictionaries.

She plucked at the collar of her shirt. The room felt warmer than usual. Or she was.

Her pile of read letters was already taller than the disorganized heap of papers still to be gone through, so she decided a break was in order. Tugging off her daytime clothes, she reached in the closet for a long T-shirt. As her hand closed over the no-nonsense garment, her arm brushed against the pink satin nightgown.

It was beautifully cool against her fingers. Glad she'd surrendered to the impulse to bring it downstairs, she let go of the handful of cotton and pulled the swatch of luxury fabric off its hanger.

She wriggled into it. A cheval mirror stood next to the dresser. At the sight of her reflection in the spotted glass, her edgy mood faded a little. She sighed with pleasure. The inch-wide straps and very low, draped neckline made the most of her curves. In fact, she realized in happy surprise, the nightgown boosted them from adequate to alluring. From breasts to hips the smooth, revealing line emphasized her small waist and the pert swell of her bottom. Below the hips, satin flared out in gleaming, petal-shaped gores.

Holding her arms out wide, Persephone twirled in an impulsive circle. The pink skirt belled. The straps, a smidgeon too long, fell off her shoulders.

"I'll bet Mack would have thought twice about dumping us at the door with an armful of homework if he'd seen us in this," she told the animated face in the mirror. Then she stuck out her tongue at her reflection. "Don't get ideas, hussy. It'll be better if he never knows what he's missing."

Collapsing in a pool of pink on the bed, she pushed the straps back where they belonged and selected another letter. At the end of two hours, she had read all of them. They were about . . . unicorns.

Some were so cloyingly whimsical, she almost gagged reading them. Others came from otherwise intelligent-sounding people who wrote as if mythological beasts were their best friends.

Persephone didn't count herself among the true believers. Of course, she believed in Buster. But that was because she saw him every day. If they ever became separated, she had the uneasy feeling common sense would erode her memories until she came to doubt the colt's existence. He *was* an extremely unlikely critter.

In the meantime, Mack was a laughingstock.

Your fault, she lashed out at herself. *All your fault. Mack wouldn't be fighting for his future if you hadn't stolen Buster.*

Restlessly, she pushed the papers onto a piecrust table she'd looted from the dining room. It had been fun, choosing a small chest of drawers here, a lamp there, and carrying them to her basement domain. Thank heaven for the elevator.

The elevator had brought her together with Mack, too. Whom should she thank for that? Buster? Fate?

Persephone wasn't ready for the notion Mack was meant to be something inescapable and dramatic in her life, like her . . . destiny. The soft eyelet quilt billowed around her as she flopped onto her stomach. What *was* Mack to her? Well, he was certainly an opportunity.

Wouldn't it be just like opportunity to come knocking when there was no way she could open the darned door to destiny?

As if her thought conjured the sound, the door vibrated with three quick raps.

Her arms straightened in an automatic response to lift her upper body from the bed. "Mack?" she called.

The door swung inward. "About those letters," Mack said. "I was feeling guilty—" He stopped in mid-motion, his body leaning slightly forward, his hand frozen on the knob.

"What are you wearing?" he demanded, his voice even huskier than usual.

Persephone glanced down at her chest self-consciously. One of the straps started to slip again, and she shrugged one shoulder hastily to keep it in place. "It's a nightie."

Mack couldn't quite catch his breath.

The gown was sensuous, satiny and pink—the pink of blushes. This woman, in this nightgown, was sex incarnate. Not sweaty, no-commitment, sex-for-its-own-sake sex. That kind could, with a little luck, be found in a stranger's bed. Instead, "Penny" was, hell, he didn't know how to describe her. Or what she made him feel.

The bittersweet flavor of a teenager's first kiss. That first invigorating stab of air after a cold, cleansing spring rain. The first ice cream cone of summer. There was such an aura of first times about her. And first times were inevitably sad as well as sweet, because they could only happen once. One chance to make it right.

At the sight of her he felt perspiration spring out over his body, a body that hardened so swiftly pain shot through his groin. A groan slipped from his throat. But the images that filled his mind weren't of bunching her satin skirt out of the way and taking quick satisfaction. In that pink thing, she looked like the virgin he was sure she was. Vulnerably curious, vulnerably eager. Ready, but not for a no-holds-barred roll across her white coverlet.

Even the bed was a setting for an untouched princess. It was narrow and canopied, with lacy draperies that fluttered as he closed the door, shutting them in together.

"Why did you do that?" she whispered.

"Why did I do what?"

"Why did you close the door?"

Whatever had been making her stiff and aloof earlier in the evening had obviously melted away. That was fine; that was great. But he had to think of a way to balance the urgency of his arousal—it wasn't just a background ache anymore—with all the gentleness he wanted to shower on her.

"I closed it to be alone with you." Resting his shoulders against the old, carved panels, he scrubbed his face with his hands. "It occurs to me that I'm taking things for granted. Sorry. That's stupid. I want you so much it's making me punch-drunk. Only jerks make assumptions about a woman's willingness or unwillingness. So I'll ask."

Bluntness might not be smoothly seductive, but finesse had never been his strong suit, anyway. At least he'd verbalized his desire, he congratulated himself, even if he hadn't been exactly coherent.

Her body stayed poised, graceful and somehow fey, half raised from the bed. Magic. She might have been under a spell, her motionlessness was so complete. His blood thundered. She was enchanted, and enchanting.

"Well?" he prodded.

Her wilful mouth trembled into a smile. "You haven't asked me yet."

"I thought I did. You need it spelled out?"

"Uh-huh."

"Will you make love with me?"

Slowly, she lowered her upper body onto her elbows and looked at him over crossed arms with a misty—hungry—blue gaze. The straps fell loose and sexy off her shoulders. She began to lift her hands to them, then, coloring, left the narrow bands where they were. "You don't have to shut the door for that, Mack."

Was she saying yes?

"I like privacy. There's always something watching in this house. I don't want it watching us." He walked toward the bed.

White hangings brushed his head when he reached the side. Her eyes were on a level with the area of his black slacks below his waist. They grew big and dazed as she stared at him.

"You . . . um . . . you . . ."

"Yeah. It's the way you make me feel."

Maybe they'd better clarify exactly how willing she was. Matters were already to a point where leaving without relief would leave him crippled with pain. But he was still capable of leaving. Barely.

His mind recoiled from that "barely" as soon as the thought struggled through the desire fogging his brain. If she said no, he'd back off. He wouldn't like it. But he could do it.

"Is the night together what you want, princess? If it isn't, you're going to have to say so. Now." Mack couldn't control the rough edge in his voice.

Sitting up, she reached her hands to his face. He could feel a pulse of desire, like electricity, in her fingertips.

"Oh, Mack. Oh, Mack. Of course I want you."

He touched her hair, her cheeks, the long, youthful throat. Her hands slid down to his hips, close to the urgent ache at the center of his body.

"Penny," he said hoarsely.

Clothes had never seemed more in the way. On the brink of tearing at his zipper, Mack stopped. Damn it, he didn't even know her real name.

"Only you're not Penny. Who are you?"

"Does it matter?" She threw her head back, the temptress of his dream, wild and willing. "Mack, I know even if you don't that making love is a big mistake for us. If we stop to analyze it, it's not going to happen."

Her eyes begged him for understanding—but of what? Did she want him to respond to the mutual need flowing between them? Yes, he could do that. Did she want him to forget about all her secrets? Well, he couldn't do that.

"Who you are matters." He tried to ignore his body's protests. "You're not some faceless sex object to me. For the love of God, what's your name?"

8

"I DON'T MIND WHEN YOU call me 'princess.' Why can't that be good enough?" Her hands fell from his hips. Helplessly, almost angrily, she said, "I'd tell you my name if I could."

"Hell," Mack muttered. He recognized the reason for her sharp tone all too well. "You want it so much it hurts, don't you?"

"Yes," she confirmed shakily.

"Me, too." He took a deep breath. "You win, princess. Come here. We'll make it right."

Persephone rose to her knees and leaned her body against him. She locked her hands around his neck and they clung for a few moments, not speaking. Slowly, she absorbed the shape of his body—his broad chest, long legs, taut muscles. The definite outline of his arousal.

She did ache for him, not just in her breasts and between her legs, but all over. Her skin shivered at his slightest touch. She was grateful that he held her, because she couldn't have stood unsupported. Her muscles—her bones—had turned to liquid.

"Please," she murmured into his neck. "Please."

A noise came from his throat; it wasn't a word, just a low, reassuring growl.

She sighed in anticipation as he lowered her onto her back. Not bothering with buttons, he dragged his shirt off over his head, ruffling his hair. Then he tore off his black pants and black briefs. Somehow he managed to undress without letting go of her completely.

As soon as he was nude, it was impossible to look anywhere but at his arousal. Mack wasn't a hairy man; his chest was smooth and sleek. Around his malest parts, though, clustered thick, dark curls. Not quite daring to touch him too intimately, she put out a finger to stroke the curls.

He made another low noise—it might have been, "Wait." Then, chewing out the words with painful effort, he said, "First times ought to be slow. Real, real slow. Special." He stopped her finger by trapping her hand in his. "We don't start there—we end there." Lifting their linked hands to his mouth, he kissed her fingertips. "Let me show you."

"Please," she said again. She didn't recognize the drowsy sound of her own voice.

Mack meant it when he said slow, she thought. Easing onto the bed, he hooked an arm under her neck. All his movements had a slow-motion, underwater feel. It was remarkably sensual. She held her breath, wondering what he was going to do next.

There wasn't enough mattress. Mack was far too big and dark and aggressively male for her narrow, feminine enclave, with its white-on-white shams and fantasy of French lace. But somehow, by half sitting against cushions piled at one end and putting one thigh under and one over hers, he managed to fit.

His legs were heavy, and warm.

"My nightie's in the way," she murmured.

His frown of concentration turned into a crooked grin. Persephone explored it with her fingertips as, one tormenting fraction of an inch at a time, he pushed the bodice of the nightgown down over her breasts. She looked down to see what he was seeing, and gasped softly when the dusty pink satin slid past her nipples. The material's silky glide made the tips of her breasts feel like velvet.

His muscular arm under her head was too firm to be comfortable, but only its solid strength kept her earthbound. Mack's touch had her spiraling into a sensual world of textures and scents. Soft satin and percale, sleek skin, a whiff of lavender from the bedclothes, the spicy musk of man.

Sinking into his embrace, she let her doubts go and simply felt.

Warm and firm, his palms caressed her breasts while his thumbs teased the nipples. The hot ache grew stronger where he touched her, as well as deeper down. Suddenly, fiercely, she wanted to be touched there, too. She raised her hips, seeking relief, and heard Mack let out a low chuckle.

Persephone didn't want slow. She wanted to press herself closer. But her skirt and his legs trapped her, and the frustration edged the achy heat up a notch. She moaned out loud.

Mack began to shake with suppressed laughter. Persephone didn't know what he was finding so funny, but she decided to do something about it. By touch, she located the gown's old-fashioned side zipper. The soft rasp of the zipper stopped his amusement so abruptly she opened her eyes to look at him.

"Don't laugh at me," she whispered. "Help me out of this darned thing."

"I wasn't laughing at you," he denied. "I was ... pleased...at how sensual you are." A tug from his large hands brought the satin confection to her waist. She had to shimmy in his grasp to get it past her slim hips. Mack leaned down the length of her and pushed the gleaming pink fabric over the mattress's edge. His gaze lingered as he straightened; his eyes held a look of wonder. "You're like a fantasy come true. But you are real, aren't you?"

"I'm real. Touch me."

He slowly ran his fingers over her waist.

"There," she begged as his hand descended further. "Hurry. Harder. Oh, Mack, I've been waiting forever for you to touch me *there....*"

His fingers trailed in a teasing circle around her pale triangle of hair. "That proves you're a fantasy. What man doesn't dream of a woman who asks for fast and hard—"

"Yes. Yes." Grabbing the tormenting fingers, she pressed them into the center of the circle. Both of them gasped. Persephone's eyes flared wide. "Mmm. Yes."

Two fingers glided over her soft flesh. Even with her eyes wide open, the sensation blurred her vision. Briefly, his dark face swam above hers.

Then his mouth crushed her lips, warm and firm, and his tongue was deep inside her mouth and it was wonderful. His other hand covered one breast. It ached for him. Darn it, it swelled for him.

At the entrance to her body, his fingers eased inside, first one and then the other. All the throbbing sensation tightened around his fingers. Persephone lifted her hips wildly. She couldn't bear this overwhelming intimacy; she wanted it to go on forever.

Mack tore his mouth away from hers. "That's right, princess. Reach for it. You can get there."

"I don't know how!"

"Sure you do. Look at me. See yourself in my eyes. Find out how beautiful and strong and sexy you are."

She heard her breath, loud and erratic, as she stared into Mack's gray eyes. The pupils were as shiny as onyx, as reflective as mirrors. She saw her face floating, staring back at her. Tousled hair, misty gaze, lips kissed dark.

"Believe in the magic," he said thickly.

His fingers thrust, met an obstruction, withdrew, pressed forward again. The hot, tight urgency in her peaked, and she whimpered, hearing the sound from far away. The onslaught of pleasure convulsed her, and then slowly, sweetly, relaxed its relentless grip.

His fingers slipped away.

"*Oh.*" Feeling light, boneless, languid, she smiled up at Mack.

He didn't smile back. She ran a gentle, inquiring hand over the dark flush on his cheeks and his throat.

"Oh," she said again. Her fingers drifted down his chest and stomach until they closed over his solid length. This time he didn't stop her. He closed his eyes, breathing harshly.

"There's still some magic left," she whispered.

He replied raggedly, "I'm afraid of hurting you. You're a virgin."

"Technically, at this point, I suppose I am," she agreed with a twinge of amusement. But sweeping her palm over his silky skin gave her another throb akin to that incredible climax. "Ever since I saw you gazing at me through the elevator grille, I've been awfully tired of virginity."

"All right, princess. I'll try to make everything good for you."

"You already have—"

Before she could finish the sentence, he gently pushed her hand aside and covered her body with his. A pressure, like that of his fingers but fuller, harder, *better*, entered her.

He was inside.

Her body had been made for this, she realized, her heart pounding again. Made to cradle his weight. Made to enfold a man. This man.

He shifted his weight to his elbows. Persephone wrapped her arms around his back, tugging him closer.

Lifting his upper body again, Mack muttered, "I'm too heavy for you."

"You're perfect for me," she scolded.

With a shake of his head, he framed her face in his hands. "We're not all the way—together—yet. You may feel a little pain now. This part'll be over in a sec." He bent his head. "I want you. All of you."

His kiss was a brush of moths' wings across her eyelids. It was the kiss, rather than his hard thrust, that stung her eyes with tears.

There was pain. Along with it came the private, instinctive knowledge that she would never be the same again. Her body was no longer inviolate. It was shared. Used, as it was meant to be used. Complete.

Lovemaking. A beautiful word for a beautiful act. Making . . . love . . . with Mack.

Snagging her feet around his legs, she locked him close.

His hands were still cradling her face. "You okay?"

"Mack. Of course."

His whole body was rigid with sexual tension. He stayed motionless except for the thud of his heart and the shallow pumping of his lungs.

"What about you? Are you okay?" she asked anxiously.

"Oh, yeah. Oh, yeah." His ecstatic smile soothed her anxiety and somehow created ripples of new desire. With a long, deep thrust, he established lovemaking rhythm. "Let's make some more magic."

SEX WASN'T WHAT SHE'D expected, Persephone decided, her breath gradually slowing.

Technique seemed to matter less than commitment to the moment. Of course any other kind of commitment was impossible.

Mack's hand brushed her back with tender strokes, and she focused fiercely on not thinking about commitment.

Every move, every part of their bodies, had been another enchantment, another adventure. Giving herself to Mack wasn't a sacrifice...it was a gift. And they'd both been the receivers.

"That was kind of extraordinary, wasn't it?"

"I thought so." His lazy voice was a burr in her ear. They were tangled together on top of the bedclothes. "Though there was a minute right when things got interesting I was afraid I'd lose it." He kissed her nose. "You're so sexy that for the first time since I can remember, the, uh, proceedings nearly finished as soon as they began."

"Was that why when we—you—that's why you just held me to start with?"

"Yeah. I was doing multiplication tables. They're a great distraction. Not the easy ones—the twelves. A guy really has to concentrate on the twelves."

She cuddled into his chest. "And I, poor deluded female that I am, hoped you were thinking about me. Unless you're fibbing?" she asked hopefully.

She found herself lifted six inches over his chest and held there in an iron grip. The amber light shed by her bedside lamp didn't soften his battered features. "I don't lie to you. Ever. Got that?"

"Yes, Mack," she whispered.

But *she* had lied to *him*—at least by omission, she thought as he lowered her to his side. She shivered.

"Are you getting cold?" he asked in a gentler tone.

"Maybe a tiny bit. Here, let's get under the covers. That is, if you're staying the night."

"Aren't we past the point of needing to ask?" He paused in the midst of rearranging his muscular legs.

"I guess we are." Persephone gave all her attention to folding the coverlet down to the bottom of the bed, and then lifting the blankets and top sheet so they could crawl in.

Mack left as much room for her as possible in the narrow space. Scrambling in second, she wasn't really surprised when he said firmly, "Let me spell it out. I don't believe in playing games. I want every night with you. Have a heart. A broken-down ex-boxer can't take stress."

She punched one superbly muscled shoulder. "Funny. I don't recall your physical condition showing any signs of strain a while ago."

"Hey, I told you, those multiplication tables are hard."

Fending off her fist by blocking it with his arm, he pressed her into the mattress. The movement dislodged the covers from her breasts. He studied them, his expression growing absorbed.

"Mack, something else can be described that way, too." She wriggled against the growing evidence that he was becoming aroused again.

He blew out a regretful breath. "We can't. You're new at this, remember?"

"What difference does that make?"

"To be blunt, if we go on, you won't be able to walk tomorrow." But he didn't stop looking. The leisurely way his gaze roamed her breasts caused the nipples to tighten into little crests.

"It would be worth it," she assured him shyly.

"Twelve, twenty-four, thirty-six, forty-eight—"

She slid one slim hand firmly around his neck. Persephone pulled his head closer while she used her other hand to cup one breast and offer it to him.

Instead of continuing to sixty, he murmured, "Know what? I love you."

Persephone started. He couldn't love her. Not when she was responsible for Buster, and Buster was responsible for destroying his reputation. Not when the brightest future she could hope for was a prison cell with an outside window. Guilt stabbed her. Making love was reckless. Falling in love was out of the question. There had to be common sense limits to enchantment.

Letting him develop feelings for her was just plain dishonorable. Once upon a time, she'd been so proud of her honesty. Now her life was shattering into a crazy quilt of lies.

"Shh." Helpless against the need to give what Mack so obviously craved, she arched to bring her breast to his mouth. His tongue came out and touched the sensitive peak.

They both succumbed to the magic.

9

MY FIRST MORNING AFTER. Persephone cast a cautious glance at her lover. Overnight, his jaw had turned dark with stubble. A frown twisted his eyebrows as he slept.

All the magic was gone. A narrow shaft of light fought its way through a crack in the window shade. Its single white beam battled with the yellow glow from her lamp, producing an unnatural color that made the room look tawdry. Her antiques looked tired—secondhand treasures. The air held traces of the musky odor of heated bodies.

The bed was a ruin. Not only had the feminine coverlet slipped completely to the floor, but last night's activities had shifted one of the canopy's rosewood posts off its moorings. They'd been lucky the whole impractical structure hadn't collapsed on top of them.

She pressed a soft kiss on the shoulder of the ferocious-looking man in her bed before easing a leg out from under him and onto the floor.

A hand clamped around her other leg. "What?" asked Mack groggily.

She interpreted the question. "After eight-thirty, I'm afraid."

Vigorously massaging his head with his other hand, Mack sat up. "Nah, not 'what time is it?' What are you doing?"

"Getting up." She tugged to retrieve her ankle, but he didn't let go. "I've got things to do. I never stay in bed this late. And you must have a breakfast meeting or a lunch or something. You did yesterday."

"I met some professional fund-raisers yesterday." He spoke impassively. "They were negotiating to keep ninety-five percent of everything people might give for remodeling the castle. I said no. They pointed out no one is going to donate a dime to a cause with my name on it. I said no again. We can sleep in. Come back to bed."

Persephone wanted to crawl back under the covers and make him forget the insult. Unfortunately, poor Buster had to be starving. And a hungry Buster never failed to go in search of his breakfast. Picturing the amateurish railings that she hoped still contained him, she said, "Thanks for the invitation, but I'm afraid—"

"Not for sex," he interrupted, the frown that had never disappeared deepening. "Just for some hugs. Or would you like to tell me what it is you have to run off to, so early in the morning?"

She stared down at his hand on her leg. It was a large hand, very capable in appearance; the back a tanned square, the fingers blunt-tipped and strong. "Telling you wouldn't be my first choice," she admitted.

"I didn't think so." He sighed. "Listen, we both know you're running out to take care of the unicorn. I admit one of my reasons for bunking down in the castle is to see your weird pet again. And I have a confession to make. All those letters I dumped on you last night— that was to show you what I'm up against, trying to get this shelter started while I'm hampered by the reputation I've developed lately. It was dirty pool. But, God, can't you trust me?"

The bleakness in his eyes made her recoil. "It's not a matter of trust. If I didn't trust you, last night wouldn't have happened. It's—a matter of safety. Yours as well as mine."

"Safety." His lips twisted into a bitter line. "Well, I can't blame you for wanting to be safe." His grip relaxed, and she twisted off the bed.

Her nakedness embarrassed Persephone. While the previous night's activities didn't bother her, Mack's mood this morning did. She'd never seen him bad-tempered before. Another first, she thought unhappily, one she didn't enjoy. Suddenly she felt a little sticky, a little sore and, like the room, a little shopworn.

"I have to use the bathroom," she murmured, and escaped.

You're running away again, she accused herself.

Her shower was no more than a single burst of cold water to rinse off a quick sudsing. When she returned, Mack was wearing yesterday's disgarded black slacks. The scowl was still in place. He glanced up from heaving the bedpost into its socket. His ominous silence unnerved her. Those hard eyes went unerringly, like radar, straight to the gap in the towel she'd tucked around her breasts.

The closet door provided a screen. Angled carefully, it hid her as she dropped the inadequate shield of the towel and dragged on panties, faded jeans and a gray sweatshirt.

Gray seemed an appropriate choice. It matched her disintegrating mood.

The mirror confronted her when she came out from behind the door. It reflected subtle differences in her appearance. Eyes big with a knowledge they hadn't possessed before Mack. Lips just slightly bruised, swollen from Mack's kisses. Hair tousled by his hands, and the pillows they'd shared. Even the way she stood had changed; she looked less self-conscious, more aware. More . . . like a woman.

Plying her brush rapidly, she worked out the tangles and snapped an elastic band around her hair.

Turning from the mirror, she bumped her nose into Mack's bare chest. "Sorry," she said briefly, and tried to step around him. He veered sharply into her path.

"You really fill up a room, don't you, big fella?" she asked with more than a hint of sarcasm.

Last night they had soared with enchantment. This morning Mack's transformation from primeval lover to incomprehensible stranger was bringing her down to earth with a thump so resounding it was painful.

Well, she'd known sleeping with Mack would end with both of them getting hurt.

He stopped her from maneuvering around him again by curving his hands around her waist. Persephone discovered her body refused to move at all. These hands belonged to her lover. She remembered them in her hair, on her breasts, gentle and then demanding . . .

"You're freezing me out again, ice princess."

"Me?" The injustice almost strangled her. "What about you? You wake up in a foul mood, and snap and growl and grab me like some Neanderthal bully not once but twice—"

Immediately, his hands fell away. "I wake up to catch you sneaking out of bed. You aren't interested in hugs.

I don't get a decent kiss because you have to dash off." He raised his hands and then dropped them. "You're obviously neck-deep in trouble. Can't you see I'm worried about whatever it is you're involved in?"

"Mack—"

"And last night I told you I love you."

"I thought maybe you'd forgotten about that," she answered feebly.

"*Forgotten?*"

"Or changed your mind. Or—guys say 'I love you' in bed all the time, don't they?"

"Not me." His words were like icicles. "To be perfectly clear, I've never told a woman I loved her before in my life."

Persephone wanted to melt through the floor. A warm, happy feeling liquified her legs . . . but some of the unstable feeling was due to squirming humiliation. He loved her? She'd insulted him by treating the statement as a bedroom courtesy.

He loved her. And she couldn't love him back. Couldn't, shouldn't, wouldn't . . .

"Then why haven't you smiled once this morning?" she rallied.

"Why haven't you?" he shot back.

"I did," Persephone admitted. "But you were asleep. You were frowning in your sleep, too."

Barefoot, he padded away from her and bent to pick up his shirt. He shrugged it on. Through the folds of cloth, his voice emerged in a muffled snarl. "I was dreaming. A nightmare."

"Mack, that's horrible."

"I met this woman, this very special woman, and made love to her. Several times."

"Was that so bad?" she asked, holding her breath.

Mack finished adjusting his shirt with a jerky movement. "Only because I forgot condoms."

Her hand flew to her mouth. "So did I. Mack, how could I be that irresponsible?"

"Don't look so tragic. It was my fault. I should have known if I came to your room to explain about the letters something would happen." His crooked smile lit his face. "That's why I was . . . mad. Mad at myself. Not because we made love." He waited long enough for her heart to beat one, two, three frantic times, and then he added, "You're forcing me to ask. Any regrets?"

The way he kept pushing the conversation back to a discussion of feelings wasn't fair. "No regrets," she told him carefully. "Skipping protection this once—"

"Twice," he reminded her dryly.

"Twice," she agreed, blushing. "Anyway, it's not such a crime."

Going to the dresser to rummage for socks, Persephone half turned her head and caught him staring at her oddly. He came up behind her and slipped his arms around her waist. His hands wandered under her sweatshirt. "Hasn't it occurred to you," he asked in her ear, "that I might have got you pregnant?"

"Once you mentioned protection—or the lack of it— yes, of course, I thought of that." She shrugged. "But I know enough about the biology of the female body to be pretty sure we ought to be safe this time of month. Relatively safe, anyway."

"'Relatively safe' isn't safe enough. Not when we're talking about you."

It would be so easy to love this man. Resisting the temptation to lean back into his chest and thighs, she pushed ineffectively at the insidious, seductive hands climbing toward her breasts. At least, she meant to push. Somehow her palms ended up cupping the backs of his hands.

Buster was probably eating the railings by now.

The thought filled her with fresh determination. With an effort of will, she broke away, jerking her sweatshirt to her hips. She pivoted to face him. Mack's eyes slid to her waist.

"If you're wrong about your biological facts, princess, you don't have to worry. I wouldn't let you face a pregnancy alone."

MACK'S PROMISE HAUNTED Persephone as she cracked open the double gates for his car. Absentmindedly, she pinched the hasp of the padlock around a section of the fanciful ironwork.

Her intention—not very well followed through—had been to keep him uninvolved. What if their joint carelessness resulted in a baby? That wasn't exactly "uninvolved."

It wasn't anything she could run away from, either.

However, while it was possible for a woman to get pregnant during a first sexual encounter, it didn't follow she necessarily would. And her cycles were regular, with predictable symptoms of ovulation. She wasn't anywhere near that particular phase right now.

Under other circumstances, it would have been intriguing to contemplate having Mack's baby. Not now. Not with Buster to worry about.

Mack stuck his head out the car window. Catching her hand, he kissed it. A swab of his tongue across her palm sent a tingle straight to the slight, precious soreness between her legs.

"The only reason I'm going to my office today is because I'm a nice guy," he told her. "I know you're trying to get rid of me. You've got my phone number if you need it. Want me to bring a pizza back for dinner, or are you willing to risk going out with me again?"

"Pizza," she decided, trying to ignore the shrewd way his eyes narrowed. Automatically thinking of the expense, she added, "Plain."

"Cheese pizzas are for wimps. Jalapeño peppers and sausage."

"Those sound like they'd put hair on my chest. Only, I don't want hair on my chest."

Giving her hand a final smacking kiss, he released it. "You've got a point. I don't want hair on your chest, either. Okay, half plain cheese and half the good stuff. Oh, before I forget. Did you read those letters?"

She nodded warily.

Instead of the comment about unicorns she was expecting, he said, "How are you fixed for money?"

"Mack. For crying out loud. I don't want your money."

Digging into his leather jacket, he pulled out several bills and tucked them into her jeans pocket. "Don't argue. You earned this wading through the letters. And maybe you'll run out of horse feed or something while I'm gone."

She knew she ought to feel annoyed. After all, she'd been supporting herself—with success until recently—since the age of seventeen. More importantly, to take money from a man struck her as reminiscent of the transactions between her father's women and their clients. But the emotion that put nervous butterflies in her stomach wasn't outrage. It was pleasure. *Mack cares.*

Flustered, she demanded, "Since when do jobs pay by the day?"

"It's an advance against your salary, all right? What a nitpicker. You're sure you're not an unemployed accountant?"

"Not even close," she assured him, plucking the money out of her pocket. She tried to press it back into his hand. "I know you think I'm destitute—"

"I can't concentrate on business while I'm worrying whether you can afford bus fare to the hospital."

"Why would I need—"

"In case you have to go to the emergency room. Accidents happen. You could cut yourself gardening or fall down some stairs. And you're too damned stubborn to call an ambulance. We both know you'd rather bleed to death than let somebody suspect you're hiding out here."

"If it comes to that, I could drive myself. I have transportation, Mack. Please, take your money back."

He registered surprise with a duck of his chin. An old boxing move, she thought.

"Where are you keeping a car?"

"Why should it matter?" she asked, waving her arms in frustration. The money flapped in her grasp. "It's inconsequential."

"Right. And you don't have any education, but can throw around words like 'inconsequential.' Come off it. Trust me with *something,* okay?"

There it was again, she thought—the tug of reality between them. Mack's honesty, his built-in tendency to help, his darned heroic qualities, kept running headlong into her life of evasion. She licked her dry lips.

"I told you. I trusted you last night. That's all I have to give. If it's not enough, I'm sorry."

The car engine filled the silence with a pulsing roar.

Finally, Mack broke the impasse. "God, I can't stand making you look so sad. Never mind. Only—the cash is yours." He added, "Let me have the luxury of worrying about you, and doing something about it."

Wrinkling her nose in defeat, Persephone shoved the bills back into her jeans pocket. "You win."

"I haven't won anything."

The tires started to roll. Against Persephone's will, her feet kept pace. "I have a van." The car jerked to a stop, and she flinched a little from his intent gaze. "It's parked behind the formal garden, on the other side of the fence."

His slowly dawning grin rewarded her. "Is telling me a detail about yourself so hard?"

"Yes," she said starkly. "I'm not doing you any favors letting you know anything about me."

"Let me be the judge of that." He shot out an arm to drag her head down for a deep, thorough kiss.

Exhaust hung in the air after his car sped away. Shaking herself, Persephone hauled the metal gates closed. They came together with a clang. The padlock, hanging from the rung where she had cinched it, bounced and produced a merry, echoing *ping*.

"Mack's got the key to the padlock!" she suddenly realized. The imprint of Mack's kiss was causing her not to think straight. She tried to forget its remaining effects and concentrate on Buster.

Abandoning the gates, she crossed the property at a fast pace. A loud squeak behind her nearly stopped her, but she decided to ignore it. Buster was her number one priority.

Thank God, he hadn't escaped. The colt greeted her with a whicker and a stamp of all four hooves.

"I'm sorry, I'm sorry, I'm sorry." Persephone soothed him as she hastily forked hay into his trough and grabbed his water bucket. Heading out of the tunnel of bushes, she tossed over her shoulder, "Hang on, swee-tie, I'll be right back."

"I'll bet Mack Lord would love to find out who his girlfriend calls 'sweetie,'" said a cool and silky voice.

Persephone almost collided with the voice's owner. It belonged to a woman who was equally cool, equally silky in appearance. Her green eyes glittered in a face framed by tastefully bobbed black hair. She backed into a wisteria to avoid Persephone's swinging bucket.

Without losing her composure, the tall brunette stepped forward and shoved away some vines. Even in the act of brushing off wisteria pods and straightening her designer suit, she was striking. Unforgettable. Persephone could remember precisely where she'd seen the trespasser before. On TV. Chasing Mack.

"You're a reporter." Accusation flattened her tone.

"Bess Tallart, the *Portland Voice*. Mack and I are old . . . friends. He's mentioned me?"

Persephone felt a slam when her eyes met Bess's. The confrontation was as basic as nature, she thought. They were like two mares, clashing over which one would be a stallion's favorite.

With a lift of her chin, she walked toward the drive-way, forcing Bess to follow. It rocked her to feel her stomach contract under the unmistakable claw of possessiveness. Mack belonged to *her*.

"Actually, I can't recall him ever talking about you," she replied with the false sweetness of artificial sugar. In the driveway, Persephone whirled and faced the other woman. "How'd you find this place?"

"As you say, I'm a reporter. It wasn't hard to follow Mack's car. He came in last night with a woman and left this morning without one. Without you. So I knew you'd be in here. Let's have a talk."

Persephone gave her a look. "Ms. Tallart, this property isn't open to the public. Why don't you slither out the way you came?"

Annoyingly, Bess's calm didn't seem to be rattled by rudeness. "My, my. Mack's little blonde doesn't like reporters, does she? What's the matter? Doesn't the idea of being in a newspaper appeal to you? That's odd. Blondes who let themselves be paid for their company usually adore megadoses of publicity."

"Paid?" Sickness invaded Persephone's stomach. "You mean like a—"

Bess smiled. "I saw Mack passing you money. How much do you charge for your services? You know, dear, I run into all kinds of men. Lots of them are desperate for what we might call companionship. I take it you wouldn't mind if they're old and flabby as long as they're rich?"

Anger—rich, roiling anger—rolled through Persephone. "Get out."

"Maybe I can do you a good turn. Mack's satisfaction is a recommendation in itself. Believe me, he's used to the best," continued Bess without losing her smile. "In spite of your unglamorous appearance, you must really be something. I'd be happy to furnish you with names to increase your client list."

"I wouldn't doubt you're more familiar than I am with that kind of business arrangement," Persephone said through stiff lips. "But you can keep your flabby old rejects to yourself. Kindly—"

A sound like fingernails dragging across a blackboard interrupted her. Alarm replaced the delicate contempt on Bess's features. "What's that?"

It sounded ominously like Buster. Persephone stepped sideways to block the other woman's view. Another scrape of Buster's horn preceded a crash of splintering wood.

Bess's perfect complexion paled.

"It's my dog." Another lie, but Persephone relished this one. "I call him 'sweetie' sometimes. He's such a cupcake. An American Staffordshire terrier. I just hate the way people label them pit bulls, don't you?"

Green eyes fixed in horror on the bushes, Bess began to back down the driveway. "You're lying."

"It's possible," admitted Persephone blithely. "But you wouldn't want to risk the chance I'm telling the truth, would you? I guess you feel about dogs the way I feel about reporters. City girl, huh? Don't be scared. Pit bulls generally aren't dangerous unless they're trained to be. Of course, even the gentlest dog will attack when it senses a threat to its owner. My dog—his name's Berserker, by the way—"

Before she could improvise further, Bess backed around the corner of the castle. Persephone followed, watching while the woman spun on her heels and click-clacked off the estate as quickly as her fashionable heels would allow.

Hooves thudded in the dirt behind her. Persephone put out a hand to keep Buster out of sight from the gates.

"Hey, there, vicious," she said, scratching behind his ears. "Came looking for a nice drink, did you? Let's go back to durance vile. I'll finish feeding and watering you, and then I'm going to have to try to get hold of Mack. He'd better know about this, before his old friend causes any more trouble."

10

SOMEBODY NAMED MADELINE answered Mack's office phone.

"May I speak to Mr. Lord?"

"Who's calling, please?"

"I'm—" What was she to Mack? Girlfriend sounded too casual, lover too personal. Too real. "I'm someone Mr. Lord knows."

"By any chance are you five foot two, eyes of blue?"

"I beg your pardon?"

Madeline chuckled. "That's how Joey, our resident codger, describes you. Are you a blonde with blue eyes?"

"Yes, I am."

"Mack just got in. Let me buzz him." In less than a second, Mack's voice filled her ear. "Where are you?"

"At a public phone next to a gift shop in Rockaway."

Her nerves jumped at the danger posed by the beach town. Nobody seemed to be looking at her, though. She threw an anxious glance behind her. Since Buster had proven once and for all his stall couldn't hold him, he was packed into her van, parked in the dirt lane. Under no circumstances was she letting the van out of her sight for more than a second.

"Mack, a reporter came to the house."

His colorful response scorched her ear.

"I agree," she said grimly. "She saw me."

"It's bad, but—"

"Not bad. Disastrous. Apparently she also saw you hand me that money. She jumped to all sorts of wrong conclusions. And I got the impression she intends to put them in the newspaper. She more or less called me a hooker. Your reputation—"

Mack told her what to do with his reputation. Then he carefully loosened his grip on the receiver before it could shatter into plastic shards. The strain in her voice tore at him. He'd known she feared discovery. Now because of him it was happening. And what about the damned unicorn?

"Did your pet stay undercover?"

Her soft breathing sounded clearly over the phone wire. He could almost hear her hesitation. "Yes, he stayed out of sight, thank goodness," she said at last.

Mack felt a stab of triumph. Finally, she was admitting the animal's existence.

"Who was the reporter?" he asked, turning his mind to damage control. "What paper?"

"She said her name was Bess Tallart. The—"

"*Portland Voice.* Yeah, I know her."

"She said that, too." A stiffness joined the scared tone of her voice.

Mack managed not to swear again. "I haven't been with Bess in a year."

"No wonder she's hot for revenge." Her spurt of laughter sounded rueful. "If you ignored me for a year, I'd be hurt enough to lash out, too."

"Nah, you wouldn't. You're not capable of spitting that kind of poison."

"Mack, this isn't the time for a discussion of past relationships. It's none of my business what Bess Tallart has been to you—"

"It's exactly your business," he told her deliberately. "I love you."

She dragged in a breath that sounded like a sob. "You don't know anything about me. I'm grabbing my things and leaving the castle. Don't chase me. Good luck with the shelter. People are just stupid if they don't appreciate what you're willing to do for street kids. Goodbye."

"Wait." He pushed his voice through the phone as forcefully as he knew how. It came out as a rough and anguished bellow. In the echoing quiet that followed, he could hear the electronic whispers of other callers, ghosts on the line. At a lower volume, he said, "Okay, go back to the castle, but wait for me there."

He could imagine her eyes, smoky blue with feelings she wouldn't admit.

"I'm not arguing with you anymore, Mack. I'm getting out of your life."

"Right, we're not going to argue. You're going to wait for me."

"What makes you think I'd do that?" she demanded.

For one thing, she wasn't bolting away from the phone. *You have feelings for me, princess,* he thought. "Does this mean anything to you?" He reeled off a jumble of numbers and letters.

"That's my license plate! How did you—"

"I stopped playing fair about an hour ago. That's when I made a detour around the garden and found your van. If you make me, I can get your name out of the motor vehicle department."

The knowledge he would do it hung heavy in the silence on the line.

"It's Persephone."

"Per-sef-oh-nee?" he echoed. She paused, as though expecting him to recognize it, and then explained grudgingly, "It's from a Greek myth. She was a goddess whose lover made her go places she didn't want to go."

Cradling the receiver between his chin and his shoulder, Mack pushed papers into drawers and scribbled notations to Madeline. "Come on—Persephone," he said, trying the name out. He kind of liked it. "If you didn't want to go where I took you last night, you did a hell of a job pretending. And I refuse to believe you're a myth. You're for real."

"Damn it, Mack," she flashed back. "Oh, damn, you've got me swearing. I should knock your block off for backing me into a corner like this."

"Great. Fine. To do that, you have to see me. I'll be there in an hour. You be there, too."

"All right." The agreement was reluctant, but he didn't think she would lie to him outright. Persephone would be at the castle.

A call to Bess's newspaper netted him an oily-sounding villain. The day editor emitted a distinct air of disbelief as he took the information that an employee of Mr. Lord had been on-site during an investigation into the Snow estate's suitability as a shelter.

"Bess is on her computer," the editor told him. "I'm composing the headline for her story now. Would you like to comment?"

"Depends on what the story is," Mack pointed out.

"The head'll be Roost for Troubled Teens or Love Nest?"

This spelled the end to any hope he had of raising money to remodel the castle into a shelter. And then there was Persephone. She'd been so sensitive to the barest hint that she could be bought. It would kill her— or kill her pride, at least.

She'd never said so, but he was almost sure she cared for him. What would happen to the love she wouldn't admit?

"No comment, you dirt bag," he said to the newspaper editor, and hung up.

In the reception area, Madeline pounced as he strode by. Before she could ask the questions he could see written all over her face, he cut in with one of his own.

"Maddy, do you remember the name of the Snow heir?"

"Percy or something, wasn't it? It stuck in my head because I wondered how my daughter would've liked a name like that...."

"But the heir's a man, right? Percy is a boy's name."

Madeline shook her crimped gray curls. "You can never tell what people are going to call their kids nowadays. Cross-gender names, they call them. Whitney, Quincy, Lindsay..."

"Madeline," he bit out, "did Thomason Snow have a son or a daughter?"

She blinked. "A daughter, of course."

"Are you sure she's called Percy?"

"No, I'm not sure. It's something like that, though." Worry creased her forehead. "I could look it up...."

Mack was already sprinting out of the office. "Never mind," he shouted over his shoulder. "I already know what her name is."

Not "Percy." Persy. Short for Persephone.

"I'M TAKING YOU HOME, Persephone."

"Brilliant. Your friend Bess and her cohorts will never think of looking for us there."

He glared down at her. She glared back. A lemon yellow van, several years old, was parked in the weeds next to the side door.

"As a matter of fact, I meant my mother's home," Mack said brusquely. "It's in northeast Portland. You'll like her. I know she'll love you."

"I can't."

"Are you saying you don't want to meet my mother?"

She tapped her toe. "Stop teasing. I'm sure I'd adore her. But I can't barge in on the woman, dragging a full-scale scandal with me. She'll hate me, anyway. Before we met, you were a respected businessman."

"Mom'll bless you. She doesn't think business is a clean enough career for a nice boy like me," Mack assured her. "Her dream has always been that I'd hit it big in commercial endorsements. Men's underwear and stuff like that. She'll drive you nuts, making you watch underwear ads on TV, for God's sake. She compares the actors' bodies to mine." He pushed her gently toward the van.

Laughter lit her eyes, then they darkened again. She balked, grabbing at a fender. "You're trying to manipulate me. Little does she know her nice son specializes in fighting dirty."

"But you know. And you know I'm not backing down. So let's get this show on the road. Or are you going to take a shot at me?" He grimaced. "Still feel like knocking my block off? You can try. It might make you feel better. Here, I'll stick out my chin."

He did, and with a furious noise from the back of her throat, Persephone clapped her hands on either side of his jaw.

"I'll show you what I feel like doing." She kissed his lips, hard. Hard enough to make him feel her teeth. Hard enough to share the flavor of desperation.

Mack tried to soften the kiss, to warm her, but she broke away and stalked to the back of her van.

"And here is what I should have shown you days ago." Yanking on the handle, she threw open the door.

The smell hit him first . . . a humid barnyard smell. The unicorn regarded him sleepily from the van's floor.

"Yeah, well, I've seen your pet before." Despite his casual tone, relief eased a tightness in his chest that had been there for a week. There really was a unicorn. He'd known he wasn't crazy or punch-drunk, as the media had been calling him, but here was the proof. "Hiya, Butch," he said, reaching warily around the horn to give its neck a quick pat.

"Not Butch," Persephone corrected him. "Buster. His registered name is Ganders Busteroo Blue because—"

"Please." Mack loaded the possessions waiting by the door into the van. TV, portable stereo, sleeping bag, cellular phone. "Right now isn't the time to discuss its pedigree. This place will be crawling with reporters once Bess's story hits the newsstands. Unfortunately, I'm a celebrity."

"I know you want to show him off to reporters, but—"

"Are you kidding?" Mack grinned at the astonished expression on her face. "I do, of course, but not until we've had a chance to set everything up right. A press conference will be the best way to unveil your little friend, as long as it's carefully orchestrated—"

"No press conference," she said thinly. "Nothing has changed. You'll have to be satisfied just seeing him yourself. Let me drive out of your life, Mack. I can't go to your mother's!"

"Then we'll crash at my house. We can hash out what to do about Butch—okay, okay, Buster," he added when Persephone parted her lips to correct him. "But you're not running away from me." Closing the door on Buster, he calmly dug his fingers into her purse, which was flung over her shoulder, and filched keys from the bottom. "I think it'll be better if I drive the van. Here, take my keys. You can follow in my car."

She didn't ask better for whom, but turned those lost blue eyes on him, and he almost weakened. Almost, but not quite. He may have strayed into a fairy tale, but there were chances he wasn't prepared to take. One of them was that she'd decide running out on him would be in his best interest as well as hers.

"Do it now, Persephone. You owe me."

"How do you figure that?"

"Have I asked you your last name?"

Small, white teeth bit down on the luscious curve of her lower lip. Her toe stopped in mid-tap.

He watched the tip of her shoe; it remained raised and thoughtful as she chewed over the logic behind his point. Slowly, her toe lowered. There was something resigned about the way the pink suede drooped to the ground.

"You found out who I am, didn't you?"

Mack cleared his throat. "Get in the car, Ms. Snow."

11

"WILL IT BE OKAY in the garage?" Mack asked, transferring paint cans to an upper shelf.

A smile pushed itself past Persephone's anxiety. Although Mack couldn't bring himself to call Buster anything but "it," he'd driven the colt to Laurelhurst, the exclusive area where he lived, at a careful speed usually associated with grandmothers on their way to church. Her mutant couldn't have suffered a jostle or a jolt.

Without having to be asked, Mack had backed the van into the garage, which was attached to his house on one side. The minute Buster clattered out and nosed around the cans and boxes that inevitably gather in everybody's garage, Mack had begun heaving the toxic materials onto shelves too high for Buster to reach.

"Miniature horses feel at home in spaces more confined than this. He'll think it's a palace," she assured him.

"His palace days are over."

Persephone shook her head, but didn't argue. She loved the castle. Mack didn't even like it, and yet he, or somebody else, would end up owning it. Her anger over the unfairness was just another wedge pushing them apart. "I packed some feed, as well as his medicine kit, so he'll be fine as far as stabling goes. He needs fresh air and grass to run on, though."

"That runt exercises?" he asked incredulously.

Buster's cream-colored sides pouched out even wider than its substantial rump. Not aware that Mack found it unpleasingly plump, the creature batted wide-spaced lashes at him.

Persephone's much prettier behind swayed at Mack as she scattered straw over his formerly pristine concrete floor. "I'm not a monster. Of course I see that he gets daily exercise."

"But it's . . . hell, princess, your pet's a tub of lard."

She looked over her shoulder, brows raised. "The fact he exists doesn't bowl you over? You don't think he's astonishing? Magical? A fairy tale come true?"

Fingering his chin, Mack said, "I suppose I'd say it's . . . sort of cute." If he wanted to keep his lover placated, he added silently.

"Well, I think Buster's gorgeous. And amazing. It makes me feel good just to look at him and know that miracles can happen. I'll bet most other people would be affected the same way. Besides, he's supposed to be stocky. He's descended from quarter horses. Miniatures are just the same as their ancestors. The only difference is they can sit in your lap."

"Thanks, I'll pass."

Apparently deciding to be coquettish, Buster lunged at him. Seeing his plight, Persephone dropped the rest of the straw and took a firm hold on the animal's halter.

"Don't tease Mack, Buster." She tied the creature's reins to a wall bracket, and then turned to face Mack. "Buster's lovable. Really. As well as unique."

"Unique's an understatement. How'd you pull the scam with the horn?" Mack tossed the last can on the shelf. The motion served to cover the assessing glance he slanted at her under his arm.

Picking up the clump of straw, she continued to strew pieces evenly.

"Buster isn't a scam. I was there when he foaled. He came out with a little hump on his forehead. Within five weeks, the hump had broken through the skin. By five months, the horn looked the way it does now."

"Con artists could have created the effect with an operation or two—"

"I've been with Buster every day since he was born. I wouldn't put it past Leo Ganders to try some kind of— well, call it surgical sleight of hand. But in this case fakery is impossible, Mack. Buster's not a fraud. He's an honest-to-gosh unicorn."

Mack rubbed the back of his neck. It seemed to him the muscles back there had been tense ever since he had run into Persephone's unicorn. "Okay," he said gruffly, "who is Leo Ganders?"

"The man I used to work for as a veterinary technician. Leo is Buster's original owner. Buster doesn't belong to me. He never did. Leo's selling him for ten million."

"Dollars? Ten million *dollars?*"

"I'm afraid so."

"You stole this unicorn."

Such an odd statement should have seemed funny. Mack was bleakly aware that it wasn't. Persephone's face had turned white as milk. "Yes. I'm a thief. And my father was a criminal, too. That's what you're thinking, isn't it?"

Marching to a wall, he slammed his fist, once, against the sheetrock, then stared at the hole his blow left.

"Whatever I think about Thomason Snow, I wouldn't say it in front of you."

"Then I'll spell it out. He was charming and dynamic and everything a girl could want her father to be. You keep calling me a princess. That's exactly what I was—Daddy's little princess." She smiled without humor. "He raised me to be pure. And all the time we were living on money he made from selling women's bodies. Isn't that a joke?"

His heart turned over at the catch in her voice. "Cut it out. The last thing you have to do is justify your father to me."

She ran out of straw. Brushing her hands across the seat of her overalls to rid them of clinging fragments, she turned. Though it was barely noon, her eyes were strained with fatigue.

"I can't justify the family business to myself. Every time I think about it, I feel dirty. The newspapers threw a lot of mud five years ago. It stuck."

"My training schedule was pretty intense around then," Mack muttered. "I wouldn't have seen the newspapers. Did they rough you up bad?"

"Let's say I stopped believing reporters were good people."

"If they claimed you were part of your father's activities, you could have sued the pants off them."

"Sure. Using what for money? Lawyers like to be paid for their time. Besides, none of the papers exactly called me a hooker back then. That's a distinction that goes to Bess Tallart."

"Whatever the press says—"

"Affects us. People are going to think the business runs in the family. Face it, I'm just bad news."

"You're willing to give me up so easily?"

Persephone didn't want to give him up at all. But had she ever had him? "How can I—"

"You're running away from the issue. The first thing we can do is show Buster to those reporters you dislike so much."

"No. No, no, no."

"Persephone, I can tell you love the animal, but you can't believe you get to keep the thing. Eventually somebody besides me is going to discover you have a unicorn. Then all hell will break loose."

Kneeling, she put her arms around Buster's neck. The unicorn whickered softly.

"I won't give him back to Leo."

Mack leaned against a wall and thrust his sore hand into his pocket to hide the fact it was clenched in frustration. "Why not?"

"Leo's selling Buster to a Hollywood type. Chasmo."

"The guy who made the movie we watched?"

"He's been convicted of mistreating his animals. You saw what kind of film he makes—those really violent ones. Remember the part where people were trapped in a collapsing skyscraper? Two stuntmen died filming that scene. He has the worst safety record in Hollywood. Leo admitted Chasmo intends to surround the world's only authentic unicorn with exploding bombs and—and—"

"Hey." Mack went down on a knee and wound his arms around her.

"Buster wouldn't survive that kind of stress, assuming he isn't out-and-out killed by a special effect that goes wrong. I know he doesn't look high-strung, but horses are!"

Mack shot Buster a dubious glance. The unicorn was right on the other side of Persephone. They made a threesome. It snorted at him and Mack wondered if Buster might have a sense of humor.

"If you say he's the sensitive type, I believe you," he said diplomatically. "In the meantime, your baby won't come to any harm here."

"How can you be sure? I doubt your neighbors will be able to ignore the odor."

Mack said something earthy.

"Exactly." Persephone managed a watery smile; his cussword described the problem all too aptly. She stood up and wiped her cheeks with a sudden brisk gesture. "Keeping Buster and me here won't work, Mack. Not long term."

"Then we'll concentrate on the short term," he answered, getting to his feet. "Come into the house. You look beat."

"I didn't get much sleep last night." Color returned to her face.

"That so?" he asked, shepherding her through the kitchen. "Some inconsiderate person keep you awake?"

"Actually, I found him extremely considerate."

Pushing her gently ahead of him, Mack steered her to a linen closet. While he piled towels in her arms, Persephone twisted her neck, trying to see his home. Once he achieved a towering heap of terry cloth, he bustled her along. Through an arch she glimpsed a navy couch. The piece of furniture spread a full eight feet, very big, very soft, and could easily sleep a couple in sinful comfort.

Lifting her eyes to Mack's face, she wondered how many times it had. She'd never questioned that his ex-

perience was more vast than hers; how could it be less?
A professional athlete, with money and a certain celebrity status, wouldn't lack female companionship.
Mack probably had to beat hopeful sexual partners off
with a stick.

Some of the letters he'd had her read had been mash
notes. The writers had plainly been dying to meet Mack
as well as a unicorn. Bess Tallart's hint of a former affair had been so broad it had stung like a slap across the
face. And Mack hadn't denied it. His hands, his lips,
certainly knew how a woman's body longed to be
loved.

Experience? Mack Lord had the technique for hustling a woman into his bedroom down cold. His palm
molded irresistibly to the small of her back. His solid
body blocked retreat.

"Am I being kidnapped?" she asked with interest.

Forget the couch; his bed was huge. It was a man's
bed, no frills, not even a headboard, just acres of
smooth, jet-black comforter and giant-size pillows.

"Yeah." Nudging her around a corner, he kissed her
neck. "You're the mythical Persephone and I'm your
lover What's-His-Name who dragged you off...
where?"

Behind a freestanding wall nestled the master suite's
bathroom. Mack leaned into a shower wide enough for
an orgy and flipped chrome levers. More than one
shower head burst into life. The hiss of water had a
hypnotic effect.

"The underworld," she said, moistening her lips.
Logic said if there was ever a time to run, this was it.
"Pluto, king of the underworld, carried her...home
with him."

"Pluto? Like Mickey Mouse's dog? Cripes, with a name like that no wonder the poor bugger had to kidnap his women."

"Cartoons were invented later." Concentration wasn't easy when he became busy ridding her of clothes.

"So what happened next, Persephone?"

"After going to all that trouble, Pluto had second thoughts. He fell in love with a nymph."

"The guy must have been a moron. A nymph when he already had a goddess?" Her sweatshirt joined her socks, shoes and jeans on the tile floor; Mack's gaze fell to her breasts. "A goddess," he repeated.

Persephone felt her nipples tighten.

"In you go." Mack indicated the spray with a wave of his hand.

Soft and balmy, the water cascaded from multiple directions. When she stepped into the shower, it flowed over her like a benediction. It washed away self-consciousness and guilt, the immediate past and the immediate future . . . at least for the moment.

"You could be taking this shower with me," she mentioned.

"Not this time." Mack looked but he didn't touch.

"The water is lovely, but do I really need a shower that bad?"

"You're all knotted up. Nothing's better to cure tension than warm water."

"Nothing?" She couldn't help the wistful murmur. Mack was sliding the misted glass door closed.

"Nothing." The affirmation came faintly through the thrum of thousands of drops striking the walls.

She raised her voice. "Sure you won't join me?"

"Let the water do its work. Close your eyes."

She did, complaining, "I'd rather be looking at you."

"You've got funny taste."

Was Mack sensitive about his looks? "Don't be silly. You could be a picture in one of those calendars."

"What calendars?"

"The kind I never peek into."

Water sluiced down her belly to wet the curls below, and then cascaded in a warm waterfall down the insides of her legs.

"If you got naughty and risked a glance, you'd know this face is not beefcake material, princess."

"I like your face. What are you doing out there?"

"Waiting for you to get tired. You need a nap."

Persephone wondered why she didn't feel sleepy. Perhaps she was too wrought up. "I'd rather talk."

"Okay, tell me some more fairy tales."

"Unicorns." She lifted her arms over her head and let the spray soothe her breasts and the sore places left from last night. The water felt good on them. "A unicorn's horn has always been considered precious. Royalty drank from cups they dearly believed were made from unicorn horn...darn, that's hard to say...because it was supposed to counteract poison."

"Sounds useful."

"Unicorns liked hanging out with virgins. That was kind of a waste, since crushed unicorn horn is an aphrodisiac."

"Damn, two things ol' Buster's good for."

"Buster doesn't need an excuse for existing. He's charming just being himself . . . uh, Mack? Can I come out now? My skin's turning all pruney. But I'm not getting sleepy."

Pushing open the glass door, Mack frowned. "You ought to be exhausted."

"Lord, what a mother hen." She smiled at him while he rubbed her with a towel. "What I am is starved."

Mack concentrated on the task at hand. As he wiped her dry, some delectable bit of her body constantly pressed against him. The soft perfection of her inner arms, or a limber leg or one small, exquisite breast. The towel slipped and *both* breasts spilled out, all white and pink and clean and . . .

"I'll start lunch. Go ahead and get dressed," he said evenly.

Leaving the bathroom, he willed himself not to be aroused. Persephone had to have at least a little time for healing after last night, whether she knew it or not.

His slightly tarnished princess needed a friend as much as a lover.

12

"HEY, SLEEPYHEAD."

"Mmm. Mack? Is it dark outside? Boy, were you right about me needing some sleep. I conked out right after lunch."

Persephone pushed her hair out of her eyes. It was wild after being slept on wet. Mack liked the way the blond strands drifted over his black pillowcase. He also liked the fact she'd slept nude.

"I told you that you needed sleep."

She threw the pillow at him. "You're not going to turn out to be one of those people who says, 'I told you so,' are you?"

"Yeah. I am. What did you think, I was perfect?" He paused next to the vertical blinds.

His face settled into grim lines as he counted three television news trucks gleaming under nearby street-lights. Well-coiffed TV reporters milled around on the sidewalk. A shabbier pack of newspaper reporters clustered in his driveway. He snapped the blinds closed.

"It's supper time," he said decisively. "How do you feel about chicken fettuccine fresh from the micro-wave?"

"Sounds great." Her smile had a higher voltage than the lamp he switched on. "Did you get along with Buster okay? I have to feed him."

"Buster and I," said Mack, "have established a working relationship. I give him peppermints left over from the Christmas stocking my mother fills every year, and he does not poke holes in my newspaper."

Persephone faltered in her beeline for the luggage he'd found stowed in her van. "The newspaper. How bad is it?"

"Could be worse," he said, sitting on the edge of the bed. He wasn't lying; nuclear war hadn't broken out today.

Her troubled glance raked him. "It doesn't say you pay me for—"

That was precisely what it said. "Let's tackle that question later. In the meantime, ma'am, we've got—what do you call them on a horse ranch—chores?"

"Mr. Urban Blight," she murmured.

A doorbell rang, and Mack clapped a palm to his forehead and glanced at his watch. He swore.

"You've got company," she pointed out.

"I'm afraid so."

"Why so glum? Unless—do you think it's reporters?" On the brink of unzipping a lightweight suitcase, she clutched it to her instead. It didn't cover much, he noted.

"Reporters are a possibility, but it's probably worse."

"Nothing's worse than reporters," said Persephone positively.

"Don't bet on it. I forgot my mother's coming over. I'm supposed to escort her to a charity dance to announce plans for the shelter tonight. It was set up before I even met you. Mom had a yen to go. . . ."

Echoing his swearword, she tore open the case and rifled through its contents.

The doorbell sounded again.

"How can I have three pairs of jeans and no shirt?" she wailed. "Aren't you going to get the door? You can't keep your mother waiting! Honestly, men!"

"Women," he retorted with a teasing grin before he ambled to the front entrance and checked through the spy hole. The person outside had familiar orange hair. The hair was standing up in a complicated and unfamiliar hairdo.

Unbolting the lock, he swung the door inward. "Hi, Mom."

Behind Jeanette Lord, a bevy of people holding microphones surged across his grass. "Knockout Machine! Is it true—"

"In," said Mack to his mother. Her stout form moved unexpectedly fast under his arm and into the house. The crowd flooded up in her wake. "Out," Mack ordered the reporters, and slammed the door shut.

"Hello, son," Jeanette said. Composed, despite the loud knocks and constant ringing of the doorbell, she slipped out of her white evening cape. Mack couldn't remember a time when his mother hadn't been bedrock calm. Shaking out the white folds lovingly, she laid the cape over her arm.

Only then did she stand on tiptoe to kiss Mack's cheek. "I should have sneaked around by way of the patio. I take it the barbarians trampling your landscaping are a result of that *Portland Voice* article this afternoon? You know, publicity's a must but you may have gone a little overboard."

"Overboard. Yeah. Want a beer?"

"Mack, really, can't you see I'm all dressed up?" Her dignified pirouette did justice to a beaded white gown.

Under the swinging hem, little white pumps peeked. "This outfit deserves the best. Don't you have any Fussy-Pussy champagne or something?"

"Fresh out. It's beer or nothing," said Mack, who knew his mother.

"Make it a beer," she sighed. Trailing him to the kitchen, she added, "What's that sawing noise? Are the reporters breaking in?"

Mack threw a quick glance at the door that led from the kitchen to the garage.

"Search me, Mom. I'll let you call 911 if they do."

"Oh, what fun. You know I never nag, sweetheart, so I won't mention the fact your polo shirt clashes with my evening dress. Have we decided not to go to your dance?"

"I'm sorry as hell, but something's come up—"

"So I see."

The note of amusement in her voice made him spin around. On silent, bare feet, Persephone inched into the room, hugging a wall. Tiny and fragile in holey jeans and one of his undershirts, with her hair in wild disorder, his princess could have been a refugee.

"Everything's my fault," she told his mother.

Jeanette plucked a beer can from Mack's grasp and popped the tab with an expert thumb. "Not that anybody's told me what's going on, but I doubt that's true. I've known my son for thirty-two years—almost thirty-three if you count the nine months he kicked and generally used me as a punching bag—and believe me, dear, if there's any fault to find, I know where it belongs."

"Thanks, Mom."

"If the paper says I'm a—well, Mack's paid companion—it's wrong."

"However," he added, fully aware his mother wasn't an idiot and had always been able to read him like a book, "we are involved. As of today, Persephone's living with me."

"*Mack.* I am not." Persephone's blush could have started a forest fire. "What's your mother going to think?"

He skirted Jeanette and the cooking island to put an impatient forefinger under her chin. "Don't be ashamed of what we have."

"I'm not," she denied, but she pushed his hand away gently. "You're the only thing that's gone right for me in months. Years. My whole life, maybe. That's the issue. All I have to give you are problems." Her gaze went to Jeanette. "Can you convince him I'm bad news? So far I've jeopardized his reputation and made him an accessory to . . . oh, Mack, to grand larceny. At least."

"A woman with a conscience." Jeanette nodded approvingly. "You I like. The last female he brought home had no scruples at all. A gold digger with eyes like ice and a computer for a brain."

Crossing his arms, Mack leaned against the side of the refrigerator. This was obviously the time for a wise man to keep quiet.

"Mrs. Lord . . ." Persephone's voice dwindled away as the rasp of two hard surfaces being rubbed together came faintly from the garage again.

Safe to join the conversation again, Mack thought. He said easily, "Since we're all such good buddies, I should introduce you two. Mom, this is Persephone Snow. My mom's name is Jeanette. Persephone is—"

"The young lady you're sleeping with." Jeanette never minced words. "Yes, son, you've made that clear. Persephone. What a pretty name. Is it French?"

His mother sipped beer while Persephone edged toward the garage door and said, "Greek. Mrs. Lord, maybe you don't understand. I'm a Snow. My father was a famous criminal."

"Was he? There's a lot of that going around. My ancestors, the MacAdams, came to the New World after being deported from Scotland. They were caught poaching. Rabbits, I believe. That was several hundred years ago, of course. Crime never goes out of style, sad to say," Jeanette philosophized. "The best way to deal with bad apples on the family tree is to recognize that everybody has a few."

"But I'm one of the bad apples!"

"Oh, I'm sure you're not. You should work on that self-esteem, dear," advised Mrs. Lord. "Son, don't we have any peanuts or pretzels to go with the beer?"

Persephone gave up. "Mack tells me you'd intended to go to the dance, and I think that's what you should do. Really."

"Absolutely not. This is much more interesting." Jeanette's towering confection of orange curls swayed as she turned to Mack. "Your former girlfriend wasn't out there when I came in, so I couldn't tell her what I think of her. But I talked to the other reporters and set the record straight on a few things—"

Mack groaned. "You didn't."

"Of course I did. I won't let nasty-minded reporters bad-mouth my boy."

He'd been enjoying the situation. His amusement evaporated.

"What did you tell them?" he asked hollowly.

"Only things complimentary to you. Millions of sports fans have seen you stripped, and we all know the idea of you paying for sex is—"

Persephone suppressed a giggle. Mack glared at her.

"Is ridiculous," Jeanette went on in a louder voice, quoting herself. "'My Mack is a god in the buff.' That's what I said. Was I wrong?" she asked Persephone.

"No, Mrs. Lord."

"Geez." Mack dropped his head on clenched fists. "Mom, leaving out the question of my—my—"

"Godlike body," Persephone put in helpfully.

He raised his head. "Behave yourself. Leaving that out, Mom, you know full well a man's looks have nothing to do with it." Mack could tell she was highly amused.

However, Jeanette blinked in mild affront. "How do you think I would know that? You're not implying—"

Persephone's slender hand grasped the knob. "This seems to be a family fight, so I'll just, uh, go take care of something in the garage. Excuse—"

With a splintering crash, a white spiral broke through the wall into the kitchen, three inches from her hand.

THE MOON HAD NO RIGHT to be so bright, Persephone thought, and the stars shouldn't sparkle. Portland was notorious for fog. So where was it?

Even without the normal overcast, her mood was dark enough to cast a pall over the crispest, most cheerful October night. Lights glowed from the building she and Mack had just pulled up to in Mack's car. The artificial dazzle should have dimmed nature's handiwork; it didn't.

"That moon could be a baroque pearl," said Persephone as a uniformed valet handed her out of the car.

Mack came around the car, tucking her fingers into the crook of his tuxedoed arm. He'd been like that—close, caring, *there*—ever since his mother had insisted the two of them go to the dance together. Her hero. Getting dressed with a large and solicitous male doing his best to help wasn't an experience she wanted to repeat.

"What's a baroque pearl?" Mack had the tone of a man encouraging his date to talk. After crawling out a window at the back of his house to avoid the reporters milling in front, she hadn't felt much like conversation during the drive to Portland's poshest downtown hotel.

She was crazy to have allowed herself to be tenderly browbeaten into accompanying Mack. But his mother had urged her to come along on the grounds that the gossip would be worse for Mack if he seemed to be hiding her. It was the only argument that could have drawn her out.

She barely glanced at the hotel's impressive facade. Her senior prom had been held here. "A baroque pearl is natural, not cultured. Not even perfectly round. Each one is unique."

He bent his head to hers. "Are we discussing pearls or funny-looking horses?" he asked in her ear.

Just as softly, she hissed, "Buster is not funny-looking."

"Maybe you're right. Mom sure fell for the little guy in a big hurry."

"I told you people would just naturally flip for a unicorn."

"So you did. She practically changed before my eyes. I mean, she was talking baby talk to it. As far as I can recall, she never even talked baby talk to me."

"We shouldn't have left her to baby-sit him," she worried.

Mack gave her hand a reassuring pat. "Why not? She was having the time of her life."

The doorman bowed them into the lobby. Persephone unclipped Jeanette's white velvet cloak and stood running nervous fingers over the tendrils of hair at her nape while Mack checked the cloak for her.

"There's quite a crowd," she noticed.

"Drawn by the notoriety. We'll see if any of them plan to open their checkbooks."

Squeezing past beautifully dressed people at the entrance to the ballroom, she rubbed against Mack's arm. Her pink strap fell down.

Mack lifted it back up. The material was smooth, but not as silky as her skin. "Those straps are going to drive me crazy. Me, and every other man who sees them sliding around on your sexy shoulders." Catching sight of Joey and Madeline dancing together, he waved. The dance ended, and Joey returned Maddy to her husband, a solid-looking man concentrating on the food.

"What am I doing at a dressy event in my grandmother's pink satin nightgown?"

"My dinner jacket didn't fit you," he reminded her. "Neither did Mom's beaded thing."

"I couldn't steal everything off her back," she said irritably. The flounce in her walk sent the other strap flying. "It was outrageous enough that she ended up having to press my nightie and pin my hair up. I felt awful taking her cloak and shoes. Look, why don't I just leave the straps down? Maybe people will be fooled into thinking they're supposed to be that way."

Although she might be anxious about her appearance, her fear was groundless. The nightgown passed easily for a dress.

A few territorial instincts rose up at the thought of other men seeing her in it. Casing out the delectable drape of satin over her breasts. Waiting in suspense for the folds to droop to her waist. Mack definitely did not want her straps caressing her smooth arms instead of being anchored in an unsuspenseful, upright position. He decided what he wanted didn't matter. Soothing her fear was more important.

"You'd be special in a paper sack. Let the damned straps fall. Do me a favor, though. If you feel the top start to follow, say something—fast."

She gave an experimental wriggle to check how securely the bodice was anchored to her braless breasts. Watching her almost gave him heart failure.

Inside the ballroom, a man turned toward them, eyes instantly attracted to the exact angle of the satin's drape. Glaring, Mack stuck out a hand to force the man's bug-eyed gaze to shift. "Hi, nice of you to come. This is—"

"Penny," inserted Persephone swiftly. She blinded the man with her smile. "So delightful to meet you...."

Whatever nerves or scruples bothered her, they didn't show. In fact, he thought, she worked the crowd better than he did.

Everyone at the dance had seen Bess's malicious story, he could tell. Ears perked up, grins froze, when people around them glimpsed Mack Lord and his scandalous blonde. Persephone looked as innocent as an angel and as sexy as sin through the exhausting gauntlet of avid stares. The pink thing clung to her like a petal on a flower, openly demure, subtly sexual. Her poise rivaled his mother's.

"Damn it, I'm proud of you," he murmured when they had worked their way across the room.

"All those deportment lessons when I was a kid," she explained. "Your guests stare, though, Mack."

"Half of them are salivating. You look good enough to eat."

She turned her head toward the end of the ballroom that contained a fairyland of ice sculptures and fancy things to eat. "I wouldn't mind some food."

"Your wish is my command, princess."

Persephone rolled her eyes, but let him take her hand and lead her to the tables. They loaded plates, picked up drinks. "Most of the chairs are taken.... Oh, look, there's a place to sit," she observed.

A small table had been crowded into an alcove, along with a lot of ferny plants.

"We can find a table with more elbowroom," he said, scanning the crowded room.

"I guess that one's too secluded. Your mother said we were to be seen so you could show you hadn't done anything to be ashamed of."

He winced. His mother's reasoning was astute, but it put Persephone in an awkward position. If people discovered her heritage, she'd feel responsible for tarnishing his reputation. She was also scared this Leo guy would find her. But she and Buster couldn't go on hiding indefinitely.

Dragging her out was the best thing he could do for her. "Princess . . ."

"However," she rushed on, "it's plain to see the hotel's underestimated the number of chairs. It's there or nowhere. You can put me on display later."

Did she think that was the only reason he wanted to be with her?

Persephone's skirt swirled into the alcove. Cursing under his breath, Mack followed.

The only couple at the table scooted spindle-legged chairs together to make more room. They all formed an overly cozy foursome in the small space.

The people introduced themselves as the state attorney general and his wife. Persephone became inscrutable behind her princess manners once more.

"Now that's a pretty dress," said Alana Lessing. She had dusty brown hair and a weather-beaten complexion. Her own outfit was the color of mud, but the older woman ran appreciative eyes over Persephone. "You look just like Grace Kelly. I hear antique clothes are all the rage."

Persephone swallowed champagne and smiled. Only Mack noticed how false it was. "It's just something I found . . . in a closet somewhere."

Then she mentioned horses, deflecting Alana into a lively discussion of local riding stables. Attorney General Lessing joined in. Obviously, the state's top law enforcement officer was a horseman.

His leathery skin creased in a grin. "Truth to tell, we drove up from Salem for this party because of the story that's been in the news. Genuine horse lovers couldn't miss out on a chance to meet a man who's seen an actual unicorn."

Mack felt the muscles around his mouth go stiff. Even Persephone's gallant smile became strained.

Mack untangled his legs from his wobbly chair.

"Let's dance," he said to Persephone briefly.

"I'm so glad you sat with us," Alana said in farewell. "Mostly people want to talk dreary politics at fundraisers. Penny, you said your name was?"

Persephone flushed. "Mmm."

Mack tugged her out of the alcove.

"You look so familiar," Alana continued, pursing her lips. "It must be the resemblance to Princess Grace. Well, enjoy your dance."

Then he had her safely in his arms on the dance floor. "How'd you know to talk horses to the Lessings?" he asked.

"Dedicated horse buffs get a look after a while," she replied. "My grandmother was into horses big time. She was friends with all the horsey set on the West Coast. I just . . . knew."

Joey walked up to them. "Excuse me, Mack." Persephone didn't miss his curious stare. "Wasn't your mother coming tonight?"

"At the last minute, she volunteered to do some babysitting," Mack said impassively.

"Oh. Well...I just wondered. Good crowd. See you."

Mack tightened his grip on her waist as Joey moved away. Her spine was rigid. "Think you could relax? This is our first dance. Another first," he added deliberately. With just as much purpose, he ground his hips lightly into hers.

Her rosy flush flamed into scarlet. "We're in public!"

"In public or in private, there are things that don't change." His flat tone didn't invite back talk. "If I brought you here to show you off, it's because I'm proud you let yourself be seen with me. Not the other way around. Yeah, eventually we have to thrash out what to do about your pet and how both of us feel about your father and a lot of things. But for now let's forget it. I want to dance with you till we're so hot we drag each other to one of the beds in the hotel. Understand?"

"Yes, Mack."

He added more softly, "Unless you're still too sore? Are you better since this afternoon?"

Her lips slowly curved into a real smile. "I'm not too sore, Mack."

"Put your arms around my neck."

"Yes, Mack."

"I love a woman who agrees with everything I say."

"Don't push your luck."

Her position stretched the loose straps, pulling the satin up and away from her breasts. Mack glanced down. Immediately, he crushed her against his chest.

"There are some sights a guy can't see and then avoid a certain condition. . . ."

"I can tell," she murmured with a demure twinkle. "Or rather, feel. Maybe we could—"

A cool voice intruded. "Mack, don't tell me you've decided to take your little blond number public. Is that wise for a man starting a shelter to save girls from a life of shame?"

13

RED WAS SUPPOSED to be a warm color. Somehow on Bess Tallart a ruby-red sheath managed to show cool undertones.

Mack ignored Persephone's attempt to wriggle free. Knowing Mack, she wasn't really surprised.

"Sorry." Joey came panting up. "I couldn't stop her."

Nodding in acknowledgment, Mack said curtly, "Take as many swipes at me as you like, Bess. But lay off her."

"Would you expand on that statement?" Bess drew a compact tape recorder out of her tiny evening purse. "'Lay' is the operative word, I believe."

At that moment, Persephone stopped hating Bess Tallart and started to pity her. It just wasn't possible to feel jealousy toward someone so wounded.

"Mack, the dance is over," she hinted strongly, pushing gently against his grasp.

"You don't have to go anywhere, princess. With me is where you belong." His arms clamped around her like steel; his square chin was set in firm, blunt lines.

"He refuses to be parted from his 'paid employee,' a blonde whose dress fell off her shoulders during the charity ball," Bess said into the microphone. "Mack, I had no idea you were a closet romantic."

"That ought to tell you something about the months we lived together," he retorted harshly. "You want a quote? Fine. This woman brings magic into my life. I do not intend to let her get away. You've got your quote. Now we'd appreciate our privacy."

"Just one picture," Bess coaxed. She crooked a manicured finger and a shaggy, bearded man popped up behind her, focusing a lens. At Persephone's pleading glance, Mack dropped his arms.

Bess's cold gaze made Persephone conscious of the fact her gown was a hand-me-down. "What's your name, little blond person?"

"That's not your business," Mack snapped.

"Are you going to say something," Bess asked, "or does Mack do all your talking for you?"

Persephone tried not to blink at the camera's lightning flash. "I talk. I guess all I'd care to say is . . . Give up, Ms. Tallart. Mack doesn't deserve this. Neither do you. You're attractive, talented and smart. Why do this to yourself? The role of woman scorned doesn't offer any graceful options."

Behind his beard, the photographer guffawed. He changed his laugh to a cough when Bess whirled to glare at him.

A brown figure hovered at the edge of the tense group. "Excuse me," said Alana Lessing, beaming at Persephone. "I just realized who you are. You won't recall me, because it was all so long ago, but I was a great friend of your grandmother's. We used to visit summers, walking in the garden at that extraordinary castle and talking horses a mile a minute. You'd tag along, such a sweet, darling girl."

"Pay dirt!" breathed Bess. "Mack Lord's blond princess is the Snow heiress."

The flashbulb popped again, capturing Mack flanked by Bess and Persephone.

THE PATIO DOOR SLID OPEN in well-oiled silence.

"How did it go?" whispered Jeanette, peering into the darkness suspiciously.

"The evening was not an unqualified success." Persephone slipped out of the white pumps and wrap, and laid them on a chair.

"We did all right," Mack told his mother. "No donations, though. Thanks for lending us your car. It's stashed two cul-de-sacs from here. We got around the reporters camped in front without a hitch."

"But how was the dance?" demanded Jeanette.

She'd changed into a sweat suit that must have been borrowed from one of Mack's drawers; above its sagging black crew neck her elaborate coiffure tilted like an Eiffel Tower of orange cotton candy. Holes in the elbows and legs indicated time spent with Buster's lethal horn.

"It was awful." Persephone sounded hopeless.

"What happened isn't that big a tragedy, princess." Mack wasn't sure how to deal with the despair he read in her slumping shoulders. So he hauled her into his arms, and held her. Just held her.

Apparently that was the right thing to do, because slowly she relaxed. Her arms crept around his waist.

But she said, "You're not being realistic about the situation." The words were muffled in his dinner jacket. "You need to dump me, and fast. God, Mack, by tomorrow the reporters won't just be calling you a—a—"

"Flake," suggested Jeanette.

"Thanks, Mom. I can always count on you to call a spade a shovel."

Persephone ignored their teasing. "The media will also imply you have ties to crime. It'll be, 'Mack Lord, whose lady of the evening is Persephone Snow, daughter of prostitution kingpin Thomason Snow—'"

"We're going to have to figure out a way to deal with the press," he admitted. "I told you, we can do it." He shrugged out of his dinner jacket and jerked loose his tie. "But not tonight. It's time for bed."

Heat crept up Persephone's throat as Mack casually snagged her hand and started toward his bedroom.

"I'll peek in on Buster," she muttered.

"Okay." Lines bracketed Mack's mouth. He released her hand after a quick squeeze. "Just don't forget where you belong."

Her gaze met Jeanette's when she turned toward the kitchen entrance to the garage. Mrs. Lord resembled a kindly witch with her black sweat suit and crayon-colored hair. She was different, no doubt about that. But her eyes were just like Mack's. Their calm gray depths reminded Persephone that this woman had survived living in one of the toughest neighborhoods on the West Coast, and had raised a fine son.

"So what really *did* happen?" asked Jeanette, halting Persephone in her tracks.

"Somebody recognized me." Persephone hugged her ribs. "I never should have agreed to go to that wretched dance. I'm so sorry—"

"You really need to get over your tendency to apologize constantly, Persephone. That's a pretty name, but it is a mouthful. I think I'll just call you princess, the way Mack does."

"I'd rather that you called me by my name." "Princess" just didn't sound the same, said by anyone but Mack.

Her forthrightness won her a pat on the cheek. "There, I knew you could stand up for yourself if it meant enough to you. However, you might as well face the fact Mack isn't going to give you up easily. He's stubborn that way."

"He won't even discuss my father. Daddy was a criminal. And from the way I've been acting, it seems to run in the family."

"I doubt he blames you for your father's actions. But tell me more about the party. Any other fireworks?"

"One of Mack's old girlfriends was there."

"Bess?" asked Mrs. Lord composedly. "Cold, isn't she? When they were living together, it constantly amazed me that my poor Mack's you-know-what didn't freeze right off." Before Persephone could do more than sputter with laughter, she continued, "What's your impression of Bess?"

"She *does* seem cold, but . . . well, Mack's called me an ice princess a time or two. It's possible to project cold and still have warmth to share inside. Maybe she doesn't know how to let people in."

"You're nicer than I am."

The tower of orange hair slid another inch sideways, and Jeanette put up a hand and pulled it off. It was a hairpiece. She fluffed out a cap of curls which, except for the color, looked much more natural.

"I'm not nice at all," muttered Persephone. She twisted her neck. A headache was pounding at the base of her skull. "If I were, I'd take Buster and get out of Mack's life."

"He wouldn't thank you for that. Not very good at cutting off people he cares about, my Mack," said his mother. "Here, let me get those pins. You must feel skewered."

With deft fingers, Jeanette located hairpins and clips, tossing them casually on the floor as she went. Persephone grinned wearily. Mack had been right. Mrs. Lord was impossible to dislike.

"My son's always been attracted by a challenge. In life, it's been boxing and then causes in the neighborhood. With women, he's gone for the ones who weren't easy to get—the self-contained, mysterious ones. I'm glad this time he's caught one worth his effort."

"Thanks," said Persephone when her hair fell straight and shining again to her shoulders. Dryness stung her lids. She knew what she had to do. "Thanks for the help and the vote of confidence. I'd better check on Buster."

"I'm very taken with him. How much does a miniature horse without a horn cost?"

"Price goes up according to how small they are. A normal mini can fetch anything from around fifteen hundred to eighty-five hundred."

"Really?" Jeanette said calmly. "I'll have to put a miniature horse on my Christmas list. Buster's been a lamb the last few hours. Very quiet."

"Probably asleep. But I need a peek. He's my baby, you know?"

Jeanette's gaze tracked the hall to Mack's bedroom. Something stirred in her serene eyes. A mother never outgrew the instinct to worry about her child, Persephone thought.

"You bet I know," said Jeanette.

The look gave Persephone a strong dose of guilt. No matter how generally adorable Jeneatte might be, Mrs. Lord couldn't relish the prospect of her son sleeping with a strange woman under the same roof.

"I can take the couch," she offered.

Jeanette smiled a little. "Don't be silly. Chances for happiness are rare and short in this life. Mack's waiting for you."

Swinging her hairpiece from one finger, she wandered in the direction of the guest room. Persephone watched her go, then slipped through the kitchen and opened the inner garage door to glance in on Buster. Securely tied to the fender of the van, away from walls or doors he could demolish, he'd chosen to go to sleep standing up. His horn dipped toward the straw-covered concrete floor. It gleamed whitely in the shaft of light from the kitchen.

Because the slightest sign that a potential playmate was near would jolt Buster wide-awake, she backed away quietly. Easing the door shut and leaning against it, she thought of her next step.

Go. Get out.

The stinging in her eyes returned. But she couldn't leave without showing Mack that she had feelings for him. Even if she couldn't tell him.

She padded through the kitchen, down the hall and into Mack's bedroom. Although Mack's laptop computer sat open on his spare, modern dresser, she could hear him in the bath area. The water was running, and his wonderful, cracked hum was massacring the theme song from "Mr. Ed."

The water and the humming stopped. "That you?"

"Uh-huh. Were you going to work on the computer?"

"Just had a couple of notes to get down. Then I remembered we had something more important on our agenda...."

Mack came around the corner, naked, one hand conspicuously holding a box of condoms. After a single glance at her face, he walked to a night table and tossed the box into a drawer.

He was frowning. There wasn't any disappointment or blame in his expression, she noticed tenderly. Just concern.

"Headache?" he asked.

She could have told him the problem was heartache, but instead she crossed to the night table and retrieved the box.

"I'm okay." Thumbing up the top cardboard flap, she pulled out a packet and studied it. "I've never touched one of these before."

He reached for a pair of briefs. "Persephone, you're more important to me than sex. If your head hurts, we can just hold each other."

"Why is a headache famous for meaning no sex?" she asked, taking the briefs out of his hand and throwing them to the bottom of the bed. "Maybe sex cures headaches."

He considered that. "We could experiment," he suggested.

His gentle tug on the side zipper loosened the gown, and a push sent the gleaming satin collapsing to the floor.

"Experiment," she repeated. His body was reacting, instantly, to hers. Heat and moisture invaded her secret parts at the sight of his swift hardening.

"A biological experiment. If you're positive nothing's sore."

"Absolutely positive."

With his hands where her hips began their subtle swell, he pulled her closer. His arousal brushed the vulnerable skin of her abdomen. But her panties were in the way.

They were simple cotton bikini panties, the color of her skin, nothing very erotic.

Her thumbs impatiently went to the sides. Mack's hands patiently covered hers.

"What's the hurry?" he asked. His voice was low and thick.

"I can't feel you right with these on. And they're too . . . not sexy. Let me take them off."

Softly, he objected, "I've got plans for these panties. Besides, no clothes you wear could be unsexy. Not as long as you're in them. Want proof?"

"I hear you like a challenge. Okay. Prove it."

She rested her forehead on his chest. Shyly she put the tip of her tongue to his dark nipple. It stood up, not blatantly the way hers would, but in subtle testimony to her effect on him.

A slow shudder rippled through the muscles over his rib cage, proof that he desired her.

But she needed to hear it. "You want me?"

"I want you. All of you."

She could give him at least part of what he wanted.

Then one of his hands slipped inside the top of her panties, along the curve of her buttock. His other hand invaded intimate territory, but from the side, not the top. The combination of the unexpected action and his slowly clenching fingers filled her with languorous heat.

"Like I said," he murmured, "I find these panties very sexy."

She didn't know what to do with her hands; she and Mack were standing and there wasn't room for any more hands below waist height. His fingers parted the delicate flesh between her legs. A whimper broke from her.

"I thought about doing this to you while we were dancing." His legs started to move in rhythm, and hers followed. Then they were revolving in close, dizzying circles. Needing something to cling to, she dug her nails into his forearms.

Mack slow-danced her to the side of the bed. His palms kneaded erotically. His fingers continued to explore. Two of them went all the way inside her. Stretching. Teasing. Burning. Fulfilling.

The panties ripped.

On the brink of tumbling into climax, Persephone gasped at the sudden sound.

"I knew I'd like those panties," Mack muttered. As he withdrew his hands, the torn scrap of material fell away.

"Mack." She couldn't seem to say anything else. Her entire body trembled with unreleased sexual tension. "Mack."

"It's okay, princess. You've still got our protection in your hand." He peeled the packet out of her grasp and ripped it open. A sheen glistened on his collarbone, the dip between his taut pectoral muscles, the insides of his arms. "You want to put it on me?"

She would do anything for him. Carefully, with fingers that were hot and felt swollen at the tips, she unrolled the latex so it fit him as closely as she soon would.

The side of the mattress butted into her legs and she fell backward. Dimly grateful that she didn't have to manage the complicated business of standing up anymore, Persephone held out her arms.

"Mack."

His body angled over hers. A fuzzy awareness that both of them were half off the bed tickled her consciousness; it didn't matter. Nothing mattered but this man.

Bending to put his tongue deep into her mouth, he closed her fingers over his arousal.

"Guide me." His hoarse whisper burned on her lips.

All of him followed where her hand led. Fitting him into that precise place made to accept his hard length sent a hot flood of sensation pulsing through her. There was pleasure in taking; there was pleasure in being taken. Giving and receiving.

"Is that how you want it?" he murmured. "Slow and easy and smooth?"

She moaned. "Fast," she tried to say. The sound was lost in her shallow breathing.

So he entered her slowly. An even thrust, and an aching withdrawal. Even though she could have sworn her body could stand no more exquisite torment, his restrained rhythm pushed the level of sensation higher and higher. Until she could touch the stars.

It was magic.

She strained to open herself to him as much as she could, and he filled her completely. Torrents of pleasure burst inside her. She screamed, *"Mack!"* as she climaxed.

Then his body shuddered with its own release. Stunned by the height of their pleasure, she clung to him. She felt as if she were all arms and legs and so-sensitive mouth. He shuddered one more time and then collapsed onto her.

"I'm too heavy," he mumbled.

She stopped his attempt to roll off her by tightening her grip. "Stay. Don't leave me yet. It'll be time soon enough."

Their breathing slowly returned to normal.

"Oh, no," Persephone said suddenly.

"What's wrong?" Swiftly, Mack eased his body to one side.

He was concerned that his heft was too much for her—damn, she was so small. The extra bulk he'd had to maintain as a heavyweight had been shed at the gym, but he still tipped the scales at a hundred and eighty pounds of solid muscle, while she couldn't be more than an easily crushed hundred and five.

The face she lifted to him wasn't white with pain. It was, however, white with horror. "Mack, I screamed. Really loud."

He relaxed, and stretched. "I heard. You were sweet."

"Sweet?"

"As in 'did things for my ego.' I like pleasing you."

"Well, I like pleasing you, too. But, Mack, think. Your mother's in the house!"

"Oh. Mom." Looping an arm around her waist, he tumbled her over him, bringing her legs completely onto the bed. The production he made out of tucking her bare body under the covers allowed him to stroke her breasts. "Mom sleeps like a log. Always has. It used to come in handy when I was, oh, around sixteen, seventeen."

"You don't say."

"I do say." He sprawled full-length beside her and got more serious about waking her responses.

"We need some sleep," she said.

Her tone wasn't really unwilling, and the push she used to fend off his hand wasn't very strong, but Mack drew back. She was new to this, after all. The pressure of so much intimacy for a woman who preferred a solitary life must be overwhelming.

However, he was wide-awake. "Things are closing in on us, princess."

"I know."

"I've been letting the press get in all the punches." He moved his shoulders restlessly. "It's time to get off the ropes and hit back."

"That's the difference between us. You stand and fight. I cut and run."

"Not everybody likes a good fight. But you don't have to worry. You've got me on your side this time. I *love* a good fight."

Rolling onto her stomach, she admitted, "I've never been able to handle other people's anger or their dislike. I was raised to please Daddy and, by extension, everybody else, I guess. When all the hatefulness crowded in on me after his death, I ran and I hid...and I've been hiding more or less ever since. After community college, I went where no one knew me. And then Buster came along and . . ."

"And you rushed to its rescue." Mack smiled at her. "You don't sound like a coward to me. Give me some credit. You think I'd fall in love with a wimp?"

Her face wasn't turned toward him, but he could sense her distress. "I think we ought to get some rest. Tomorrow's not going to be an easy day," she mumbled.

A twinge of disappointment wormed through him when she didn't say she loved him in return.

He wanted her to go to sleep happy. "How do you feel about the castle, anyway?" he asked, seeking a subject that would take her thoughts away from her troubles.

"Well, I quake at the thought of having to clean it," she answered evasively. "Obviously I couldn't afford to keep it up properly. I don't know. Before I found out I'd goofed with the taxes, it never occurred to me the castle would ever belong to anyone else. And now . . . when will the winning bid be decided?"

"Tomorrow."

"Ouch."

"Does the prospect of losing the place hurt so bad?" he asked softly. "I expect my bid to be accepted. Would you like me to give the castle back to you?"

She raised her head and looked at him with eyes like blue saucers. "You'd do that?"

Leaning over, he kissed her. Every ounce of love he had went into it. "Does that answer your question?" he said.

"Then what happens to all those teenagers who need help? No, Mack. Thanks, but the castle was run all those years on money earned by women who fell into prostitution. It'll be just fine if the old Snow place becomes a shelter to save kids from lives like that."

"You're a very sweet princess, you know that?"

She dropped her gaze. He really had to teach her how to take a compliment, Mack thought.

"Can it really be made into a shelter?"

"With enough renovation. I can afford to buy the castle. Remodeling costs would stretch my resources past the breaking point. Unfortunately, donations won't come through as long as I'm associated with the project. Right now my name is Mudd. With a capital M."

"But difficulties only bring out the scrapper in you, don't they?" she asked. "You're going to fight for the funding to make it work."

"That's how you win."

"Losing this one won't make you a loser, Mack."

"Giving up would. I'm not going to sit still and take the kind of abuse we've both been given." He lifted a strand of her hair and played with it. "Let me bring Buster out into the open."

"We've already talked about this—"

"I'm not asking to save my own rear end."

She buried her head in his pillow. "I know. The shelter will be wonderful if you can bring it off."

"I happen to agree, but that's not why I want to get you two out of hiding."

"It's not fair that people think you're—"

"A flake," he said dryly, quoting his mother.

"You have every right to resent—"

"Hold on." Mack tugged gently on her hair to bring her face close to his. "You're not listening, princess. I'm a little concerned for you. In fact, a lot concerned. How long do you imagine you can keep on ducking your head under the sand? I'll help you all I can, but let's get real here. We can't keep Buster a secret forever."

"No." She shook her head. "We can't."

"I learned a lot about publicity when I was a boxer. The right kind of press conference will make all the difference. Trust me. I can handle the announcement in a way that will protect you and Buster...."

Persephone stopped listening. He couldn't protect them. No one could.

14

MACK'S BREATHING FINALLY had the rhythm of an idle engine—quiet, steady, unfaltering. Persephone watched his still silhouette. It had taken a long time and a few more broad hints that they both required rest, but he was sleeping.

The need for slumber dragged at her own eyelids. There were limits to how long she could go on sheer determination.

Determined she was, though. As attractive as the prospect of wallowing in dreamland might be, she couldn't stay in Mack's house while her presence destroyed his life. Love didn't behave that way. And, oh God, she loved him.

How could she help it? He was an impatient man who lavished patient attention on a lover, a rough man who never showed her anything but incredible tenderness. He was all the loving she'd missed in five long, dry years of self-enforced loneliness.

And she couldn't stay. Not without exposing him to the threat of being charged as an accessory to her crime.

Gently, she touched the dark hair sweeping back from his forehead. It felt crisp under her fingers. As soon as she withdrew her hand, it sprang back into shape, as if denying her fingers had ever caressed it.

She'd said goodbye to Mack the best way she could. Making love had been her farewell. It would be foolish to leave a note. Really dumb. She and Buster didn't have time. Every minute they lingered put Mack and his mother into more danger. . . .

But somehow at the last moment she couldn't leave without telling him how she felt.

Writing paper might be anywhere. She didn't have the vaguest idea where to look. Cautiously, she tucked Mack's computer under one arm. Would the machine switch off if the top got closed? Unsure, she left it open. The briefcaselike contraption was horribly awkward to carry in that position, but she managed it.

Gathering clothes and purse under her other arm, she tiptoed out of his room and down the hall. Inside the guest room, Jeanette didn't stir. Persephone headed for the kitchen.

When she turned on the faucet, it gushed water, thank God quietly. A splash of cold water on her face shocked her only partly into wakefulness. Dressing took a long time with her clumsy, sleep-deprived fingers.

A wary peek through the miniblinds convinced her that the media people had at last given up and gone away. Bent bushes and trampled flowers bore mute witness to the reporters' indifference to Mack's landscaping. She chewed on her lower lip. Mack's good name meant something to him. How long could he love her, when she and Buster were the cause of the avalanche of negative attention that had dropped on him?

The computer's cursor flashed. Its mesmerizing light almost accomplished what exhaustion hadn't. As a porcelain knob dug painfully into her hip, she realized she was sagging against a cabinet.

Pinching her arm to wake up, Persephone set her fingers to the keys.

"Mack. Life isn't a fairy tale, full of happy endings. I love you. I can't stay and cause you more trouble. Buster says bye."

The phosphorescent blue letters glowed at her mockingly. As a letter it wasn't much, she thought, reading it over. It didn't tell him about the pain she felt for the pain he was going to feel. Or the anguish she felt for herself.

"P.S.," she typed, "I do adore your mother. Say goodbye to her for me. If you decide to hate me for leaving, I will understand."

She wanted to write *I love you* one more time, but that would have been like begging for pity. Instead she left the computer open and humming faintly on the counter. Taking her purse, she let herself into the garage.

Buster blinked awake. His questioning whinny shrilled much too loudly in the silence. Persephone ran to his side, digging in her pocket for a dried apple slice. Putting her hand to his mouth, she let him nibble it from her palm while she unhitched the rope tying him to the bumper.

"Hush, now, sweetie. Into the van. Persephone has to clean up after you."

A broom and a big plastic lawn bag helped her erase every physical trace of Buster's presence. After heaving the filled bag into the back of the van, she sighed. A certain eau de horse still pervaded the garage. There was no fixing that. She couldn't hose the concrete. Nor could she return to the kitchen and paw through Mack's cabinets for air freshener. It would make too much noise.

Once they were gone, no one could prove a stolen animal had ever stabled here. There would be nothing to tie Buster to Mack or to his mother. Even the undeniable fact that he had claimed he saw a unicorn couldn't be construed as a crime by the most zealous district attorney. The Lords would be safe from prosecution. The sooner the better.

She had to get Buster out. Fast. Time was running out.

She pushed the button that operated the garage door. The excruciatingly slow opening was accompanied by a rumble that had her peering at Mack's bedroom window as she backed the van onto the driveway.

A light blossomed at the edges of his blinds.

Hopping out of the high front seat, Persephone ran to punch the button again, and ducked under the closing door as it came down.

A burly figure loomed out of the shadows between her and the van. Buster's horn glinted, visible through the open door on the driver's side.

"If it isn't our Persy!" marveled Leo Ganders. "What have you got in the van, Persy? Something that doesn't belong to you?"

Skidding to a stop, she swallowed her shock and said resignedly, "Hello, Leo. How'd you find me?"

"Drove up from L.A. as soon as I saw news reports about some athlete who met a unicorn. Took awhile to find out where he lived. Then I got into Laurelhurst and mingled with the reporters on the front lawn." More lights flicked on in Mack's house.

"Mr. Lord didn't know I had Buster. He's not part of this. He's not."

"I don't give a—" Leo spit out an obscenity "—about this Lord. But *you*..I'll nail your sweet little hide to a wall, you do-gooding busybody. Do you know what I've been through with Chasmo the last month, putting him off, keeping him from suspecting anything while I waited for some sign of Buster? You're going to pay, sweetie cakes. I'll make sure you spend the next ten years in jail."

The front door slammed open. "Persephone? What the—" Mack's shoulders filled the frame.

Things suddenly happened very fast.

He hurtled into the yard. Leo took one look at Mack steamrolling in his direction and held up his hands in surrender.

The ineffectual gesture did nothing to deflect the juggernaut barreling toward him. No wonder he was terrified, Persephone thought. Mack would have scared someone a lot braver than Leo. He was naked to the waist, his fists were bunched and a scowl painted lines on his face. The fitful light from the street exaggerated his already-imposing muscles, causing a primitive thrill to tingle along Persephone's spine.

She pulled herself out of her fascinated stupor. "You aren't getting dragged into this, Mack," she called desperately. "I won't have it, do you hear?"

Retreating from Mack, Leo didn't even seem to notice when she jerked open the van door and jammed herself into the seat. She gave Buster a hearty shove, and the colt backed out of the crevice between the bucket seats, obligingly folding his legs foal-fashion on the carpet.

"Persephone! Wait!"

She hooked the van door closed. Her grasp slipped on the gearshift. After a seeming eternity that probably lasted two seconds, the transmission crunched into gear.

Mack's face appeared in the side window. Surprise and anger distorted his strong features into a harsh mask. His gray eyes bore into hers.

Tearing her gaze away, Persephone backed the van out of the driveway. There was nothing to say. And no time to say it.

She took the backward curve into the street far too fast. Rubber screeched and the steering wheel dragged against her grip. Forcing the vehicle straight took all the strength in her upper arms.

Buster nickered. Out the side window, she saw Leo gesticulating wildly. And Mack . . . Mack's expression was frozen in that fierce grimace. Did he look like that when he fought? Was he hating her already?

His arm lifted and his hand opened in a silent gesture. Love? Farewell?

"Goodbye," she whispered.

Mack watched the woman he loved drive out his life. He wanted to go after her—to shake her silly and demand what the hell she thought she was doing by running away. But he already knew.

She thought she was protecting him.

She'd said it over and over, and he hadn't listened. Hadn't made her understand that he took her fears seriously. No, he'd been so busy planning how to fix things . . . that he'd failed to win her trust.

The only way he could help her now was to keep the ogre in his front yard away from her. Leo. That was the guy's name.

Turning, he strolled toward the cowering figure. "Leo," he called in a falsely amiable tone. "I've heard a lot about you."

MASHING THE TOE of her sneaker on the gas pedal, she shot Buster a quick glance. A passing car's headlights lit the van's interior. Buster's brown eyes sparkled, his nose tilted at an alert angle. Washed with silver, the horn waved like a sword as he tossed his head. He whickered again, happily. The careering speed seemed to agree with him.

"You are one juvenile delinquent unicorn," she told him, turning her attention back to the road. "Oh, Buster, now where do we go?"

Persephone steered a fast course to the closest busy street. Then she slowed and drove in strict accordance with the speed laws into downtown Portland.

As she entered the city dawn slowly replaced night. It seeped through canyoned streets and dodged around corners with the tentative quality of a cat not quite sure of its welcome. The bridges spanning the Willamette River curved and twisted in the slowly spreading light like modern sculptures.

Most buildings were shut up tight. The police stations, though, were open. Persephone knew what she had to do.

Another hour, she decided. *One more hour to be with Buster before I never get to see him again. Before there's nothing left to think about except how much I'm going to miss Mack.*

A neon parking lot sign flashed, and she pulled in. A few other vehicles dotted the bare cement, but no people. As soon as her key turned in the ignition, the heater died. Cold air swirled in. Buster clambered to his hooves and clattered forward to put his chin on her shoulder. His horn grazed the windshield.

He snuffled in her ear.

"Yes, I love you, too." She stroked his nose. "But we can't stay in the front seat because you, my precious, are incredibly conspicuous. Come on. I'll feed you and then we'll lay down on the floor in the back and you can keep me warm."

Once he ate, they curled into a space too small even for a tiny horse and a woman who'd stopped growing at five feet two. It didn't help that Mack's possessions, left in the van, took up a certain amount of the available space.

The police would see that he got the sleeping bag and electronic gadgets back, she comforted herself. His cellular phone dug into her back. Pushing it out of the way, she spent the last hour she ever expected to have with Buster braiding the unicorn's wiry mane. Despite herself, drowsiness gradually became an overwhelming black cloud. She went to sleep remembering Mack's hair, where her touch had been erased the moment her hand left it.

A WHIRRING NEXT to her ear woke Persephone.

She jolted into a sitting position. Buster shook himself all over and clambered to his hooves.

It was late—midmorning, at least, from the sounds of car motors roaring and doors slamming in the rest of the parking lot.

The whirring repeated itself.

"What in the world?" Persephone wondered, pushing her hair out of her face. Patiently, mechanically, the whirring began again.

Insatiably curious, Buster dipped his head and sniffed at Mack's car phone.

"Oh, of course." Relieved to identify the source of the noise, Persephone put out her hand and then withdrew it. Logic said anyone calling Mack's phone probably wanted to talk to Mack.

Making up her mind to ignore the caller, she patted Buster and walked bent over to the front of the van. Time was up. As essential as it was to keep the unicorn safe, it was even more urgent to let the creature go back to Leo—for Mack. He was determined to start the shelter. For the shelter to succeed, the world had to be shown he really had seen a unicorn.

Making a difference in his old neighborhood defined him as a man. The man he was had changed her life forever. She had to help. It was impossible for her to leave him slowly twisting in the wind, his reputation damaged beyond repair.

More than most people, Thomason Snow's daughter had experience in the importance of a reputation.

A quick brushing helped restore her hair to neatness. Her toothbrush was in her purse. Running it dry over her teeth might not accomplish much in terms of hygiene, but it made her feel less grungy. Not better. Persephone wasn't sure she'd ever feel better again.

The phone continued to ring. Whoever was on the other end of the line seemed to possess superhuman persistence. The whirring went on, and on. And on.

Finally, Persephone couldn't stand it anymore. Reaching into the back of the van, she grabbed the unit and said, "Mack's not here."

On the brink of tossing the phone right back, she heard a deep, throaty voice say, "Persephone, so help me, if you hang up on me, I'll—"

Only one man had that rusty, take-charge voice. "Mack?" she choked.

"Have I got your attention? Good. First things first. I don't hate you. I could never hate you. Have you got that?"

"Mack, please, we have to end it. We weren't meant to work out, you and me. Fate had other ideas." Closing her eyes, she said words she didn't want to say. "Let me go."

"Fate is a bunch of bull. Listen to yourself. God, princess, you're suffering from sleep deprivation or something."

"Or something," she agreed wryly. Just hearing him gave her a large infusion of hopeful energy. Which was dumb, dumb, dumb. "How's Leo?"

"Leo's just dandy. He'd like to talk to you, too."

"I'm sure he would," she muttered, mystified. Actually, she'd expected Leo to be in intensive care. "Mack, I'm glad you didn't beat Leo to a pulp. I'm glad you don't hate me. But, uh, I'm busy right now turning myself in at the nearest police station, so—"

"You don't need to do that."

"There aren't any alternatives. Even though they'll have to turn him over to Leo and Chasmo, the police will do whatever can be done to protect Buster, and the whole thing will be public so you'll be in the clear. I've thought it all out."

"So have I. There's a law enforcement officer here in my office. You can turn yourself in to him." He recited the address. "Can you find it?"

"I could if I were going to look for it. But I'm not. The point is for me to surrender Buster far away from you. Let me keep a little pride. I want to do this in a way that doesn't land you in jail, too. Don't tell anyone you ever saw Buster more than once."

"Princess." For a moment, she thought she'd convinced him. Then he said gruffly, "Too late. I've already confessed. You going to leave me to face the music alone?"

GUILT. MACK KNEW IT WAS his best chance of bringing his sweet criminal of a lover to his office, and he felt bad for using it on her. But under the circumstances, what other choice did he have?

I love you. Her feelings had glowed from the screen of his computer. She loved him . . . but she didn't trust him enough to stay. And guilt, not trust, would bring her back.

If she came back.

Hanging up the phone, he sat at his desk in brooding thought. All the elements for a publicity coup were in place. Nodding sharply, he levered himself up and strode into the outer office.

Jeremy Lessing broke off his polite conversation with Madeline. "Will she be here? With the unicorn?"

"She'll be here." He hoped.

15

PERSEPHONE WALKED into Mack's office building with Buster on a leash.

"Psst!" A hand reached out and pulled her rapidly into a waiting elevator.

"Hello—Joey, isn't it?" She shortened the leash to get Buster to follow.

"We didn't expect you so soon. Well, come on, I guess we better go upstairs."

Buster reared, his hooves clawing the air. "He's not really built for elevators," she explained to the elderly bald man.

"I can see that. Geez, Mack really did see a unicorn!"

She raised her brows. "Did you doubt his word?"

"Well, uh, no. That is, yeah. I sort of assumed it was a joke, you know?" Joey kept sliding awed glances at Buster.

When they got off on the twentieth floor, he peered left and right before he motioned frantically with one arm. "Quick! This way."

"What's going on? Buster and I are here to give ourselves up. Secrecy is bananas at this point—"

Joey eased a patronizing glance at her, at the same time keeping one eye on Buster. The effect was rather walleyed. "You don't know anything about handling the press, do you? Boxing gives you a lot of practice in that. Don't worry. Mack's taking care of everything."

"The press?" Her question was sharp. Buster flattened his ears back. "What have reporters got to do with this?"

"Everything," Joey said simply.

They arrived at an unmarked door, which Joey pushed open. He herded her in. Several people looked up at her entrance with Buster. None of them was Mack. "Are you Madeline?" she asked faintly. "And Attorney General Lessing. Is this Mack's office? Where's—"

"Ms. Snow." Mack's secretary smiled at her. "You look like you could use something to eat."

"Yes, thank you."

"I'll go see what I can muster up."

Lessing knelt and ran his hands over Buster's forehead. "What a beauty." The hushed voice would have been appropriate in church. "He's like a legend come to life. It makes you—humble. May I touch the horn?"

"Sure." She waited while the attorney general rubbed Buster's horn with a cautious fingertip. Then she began, "I don't know what Mack's told you, Mr. Lessing, but he's got nothing to do with me kidnapping Buster. Nothing at all—"

"What's his name?"

She interpreted his question. "Ganders Busteroo Blue. As I was saying, Mack is completely innocent of—"

"Ah. Blue because of the smoky undertone to his white base coat." The technical terms came easily from him. "Busteroo because . . ."

Persephone bit back her impatience. Lessing had a one-track mind. Once, she would have been thrilled at his absorption in the unicorn. But she was here to clear Mack, not share an obsession. Bowing to the inevitable, she explained, "His sire is Billy Busteroo. The dam's Little Queenie Mamselle. They're both ribbon winners at Ganders, Inc., which is a breeding operation in Orange County."

"Yes, I hear from Mack that Mr. Ganders is the actual owner." He gave her a penetrating glance.

It was the moment of truth. "That's right," she said, with a gulp. "And Leo Ganders is in the process of selling Buster to Chasmo. He's—"

"I'm aware of Mr. Chasmo's track record with animals. Appalling."

There didn't seem to be anything she could say to improve on Lessing's opinions, so Persephone watched him carefully examine Buster. But her patience had run out. Not seeing Mack hurt like a gaping hole in her heart. "Where *is* Mack?" she asked.

"Attending to a few details," Lessing said vaguely.

His fingers were reverent. Coy as a coquet, Buster responded by tossing his braided head and swishing his tail.

Bewilderment rapidly built up in Persephone. She'd come at her lover's call to stand by him—but he wasn't anywhere in sight. Next ought to come her arrest. Instead, the state's chief law officer seemed more interested in crooning to Buster.

"What's going on?" she demanded.

"Ah, nothing. That is, there's nothing my office can do about Mr. Ganders selling Busteroo, Ms. Snow." He spoke with lawyerly precision. "Busteroo isn't your unicorn. Much as I concur with your assessment of Mr. Chasmo's unique lack of qualifications to be this magnificent animal's caretaker, I can't interfere. Unless, of course," he added thoughtfully, "the unicorn suffers some harm while under Mr. Chasmo's ownership."

"That would be a little late for Buster, don't you think?" Her frustration seeped through.

"Yes," he admitted. "But that's the way the law works. An officer of the court can't deny a person the right to own a thing just because the probability is that said person will abuse it. I cannot assume someone is going to commit a crime. First the crime, then the punishment."

Persephone smoothed the cream-colored braid. "Buster isn't a *thing*."

"I don't think so, either. He's a—a—a by-God miracle, that's what he is. I am sorry I can't order that he stay in your care, Ms. Snow."

"I understand. Are you going to put me in jail?" A smile came out of her last reserves of courage. "I'll come quietly."

The twinkle in his eyes was pure country boy. "As far as I've been informed, no warrant's been issued for your arrest. If I were you, I'd be trying to make my peace with Mr. Ganders and Mr. Chasmo. They're the ones who can file charges."

"That settles that. Leo wants me locked up."

"Mr. Ganders sounds like a charmer," said Lessing wryly.

"Oh, Leo's just Leo." She shrugged. "I guess most people have a temptation they can't resist. Selling Buster down the river for easy money was his. I guess wanting to protect Buster was my temptation." So was loving and trying to protect Mack. "I want Mack. Am I allowed to see him?"

Lessing's shaggy eyebrows rose. "Why not?"

But then Madeline returned with candy bars and coffee and joined Lessing in making a fuss over Buster. Wrenching the wrapper off a chocolate bar, Persephone repeated in a louder voice, "I want Mack!"

"Glad to hear it." Suddenly he was there, just behind her. Disconcerted, she swiveled to face him.

Then Joey peered from the door. "It's time," he hissed.

"In a minute," answered Mack, frowning. "Princess, don't tell me that's your breakfast. To think you once swore to me you didn't indulge in junk food. What a whopper."

His eyes were all over her, the way Lessing's hands had gone over Buster. Knowledgeable, intimate eyes. Emotion blazed in them. Not just anger. Furious concern. The moment should have been anticlimactic. After all, she'd already written her goodbye. She'd run away. It was over. How to run away and not look back was her speciality. The rules were clear-cut. Over was *over*.

But apparently Mack played by different rules.

"We can spare a minute for Persephone to finish," he said buoyantly.

"I'm done," she mumbled, swallowing a lump of chocolate. "What's going on, Mack?"

"It's show time." His harsh face lit with the joy of battle. "Are you ready?"

"Ready for what?" she asked, confused.

"The gentle members of the press."

"Oh, no."

"I'm afraid it's 'oh, yes.'" He smiled encouragingly. "Trust me. It won't be so bad."

"Says you," she retorted. "You went ahead and called a press conference? Well, you confront them. I can't. I won't."

In a coaxing tone, Mack said, "Persephone . . ."

"Can't you understand?" she spat. "I'm *scared*. It was proven conclusively five years ago that I don't handle the press very well. Very well?" she repeated bitterly. "They ripped me to shreds. There's too much at stake here. Buster's fate. Yours. You can't make me go out there in front of those reporters."

The room abruptly narrowed to just the two of them as Mack bent and put his face next to hers. "No, I can't make you. But I'm sure—*sure*, princess—that you can handle anything you really want to. You were a kid five years ago. Now you're a woman. Yeah, life roughed you up pretty bad." His hands curved around her shoulders. "But the experience gave you strength, and you're the only one who can't see it. All the running you've done lately has been to protect Buster. And me." He shook her gently. "I'll give you hell for that later. For now, Persephone, you'll have those reporters eating out of your hand."

Slowly, she shook her head. "That's not me you're describing. You're talking fairy tales again."

"Bull, princess. If you won't believe in yourself, believe in me. You don't have to run away this time, because I'll be in your corner."

Trust me, his eyes, his posture, everything about him said. "Have I ever told you that you fight dirty?" she asked helplessly.

"As a matter of fact, yeah."

"Okay, I'll do it. But you'd better be right."

"I'm banking my future on it."

Taking a deep breath, she put a hand in his and reached for Buster's leash.

Opening the door for them, Joey gave her a thumbs-up signal. "Sock it to 'em!"

"By the way, where's Leo?" she thought to ask Mack, over her shoulder.

"Out there, of course. Don't worry. I turned my mother loose on him. He hasn't been able to get a word in edgewise since dawn."

"Out there" was a media circus. Mack's outer office was large, but it barely contained the swirling, chattering crowd of reporters. Curving lights glared down from the tops of stands. Also bright were the spotlights of Minicams riding on cameramen's shoulders. Persephone couldn't make out Leo in the throng. The roar of too many people shouting at once didn't subside as she stepped out. However, the babble changed to cries of, "Ms. Snow! Persy! Is there any truth to the rumor that—"

With a tug on the leash, she brought Buster forward.

Utter silence fell.

Then a soft sigh floated through the group.

"God in heaven," said a distinguished man, familiar from nature programs on the local PBS station. "What is it?"

"Ladies and gentlemen," Persephone got out in a reasonably clear, steady voice, "it's my pleasure and honor to introduce Ganders Busteroo Blue. I'm thrilled to announce that Buster is precisely what he looks like. He's a unicorn."

The tiny colt froze as flashbulbs popped and sharp questions flew like bullets across the room. His tail twitched in a rhythm Persephone recognized. She walked him quickly to a spot next to a mass of microphones where papers had been laid down on the floor.

"Oh, gross," Bess Tallart's voice echoed above the noise of the crowd.

"As you can see," Persephone said in hasty defense, "Buster is a *healthy* unicorn."

An explosion of laughter rang out. The shouts continued, but in a friendlier fashion.

"Is it just coincidence that you're revealing your unicorn on Halloween?"

"It's Halloween?" More flashbulbs popped. "To tell you the truth, I completely forgot."

The barrage of questions continued. Answering them, she went over Buster's lineage, the way his horn had grown as if by magic, and highlights from his recent past.

"The idea of private ownership of this unique animal is a travesty of nature. Buster is really a gift for the entire human race."

"Oh, no, you don't! That's my unicorn!"

Persephone sighed. Leo pushed his way to the front of the crowd. Behind him, Jeanette held her hands up in a "I held him back as long as I could" gesture.

"It's okay," Mack murmured at her side. "Reporters are predictable. Listen."

"How about it?" Demands were flying from all directions. "What are your plans for the unicorn? Will the public have access to it? Are you giving it to a zoo?"

A wizened man wearing large black spectacles and a beautiful suit, and carrying a huge briefcase, shouldered his way through the reporters.

"Mr. Ganders is incorrect," he said, in a guttural, New York-flavored voice that didn't need volume to be heard all over the room. "This animal is the exclusive property of my client."

"Who's that?" asked a woman with no makeup, a severe haircut and a daunting air of self-assurance. She wore her glasses on a chain around her neck.

The wrinkled man swelled. "My client, madam, is none other than Chasmo!"

The reporters' mouths fell open on cue.

The woman promptly linked her arm through his. "In that case, I'm delighted to meet you. I represent the Department of Zoology at the University of . . ."

"Mack!" Persephone had to scream faintly to be heard across the bedlam, though he was beside her. "How did all these people get here?"

"I called them." His hard gaze clashed with hers.

"Oh." She racked her brain for something to remove the tension between them.

"You're supposed to tell me how brilliant I am."

As far as she could see, his press conference had dissolved into chaos. A number of the press had surrounded Leo, Chasmo's lawyer or theatrical agent or whatever the small man was, and the lady from the university. Some photographers were snapping pictures of Buster, who was beginning to toss his head in distress. His brown eyes had a glazed look from all the intense lights.

"Of course, you're brilliant!" she shouted. "But Buster's had all he can take!"

"Attention, everybody!" The mikes magnified Mack's throaty voice into a harsh bark.

The uproar died down.

"Ms. Snow wishes to point out some facts," Mack continued, and motioned Persephone forward.

"What do I say?" she muttered as she approached the mikes.

"You figure it out. You're the one who told me Buster would win over everybody's heart."

Taking a deep breath, she burst out, "Look at this little guy!" A thrust of her hand turned heads toward Buster. His labored breathing carried clearly over the jerry-built public address system. "This is what too many flashing lights and too much noise do to a high-strung animal. I've been told that Chasmo expects to exploit this unicorn by starring him in movies filled with dangerous special effects. Will all of you consider what that kind of stress would do to Buster?"

She sidled away from the mikes. Despite the butterflies in her stomach, she was satisfied she'd done the best she could. From the looks of the reporters, who ranged from awestruck to thoughtful to downright gleeful as they converged on Chasmo's representative, it might be enough.

"Let's get out of here." Mack put an arm firmly around her waist.

"Buster—"

"I just had a word with Lessing. Buster's out of your hands, Persephone."

"But who'll take care of him? That zoologist's hardly looked at him. She—"

"That's not a professor from any Department of Zoology. She's a state university system lawyer. This place is crawling with lawyers. They're not going to let you get near Buster again."

"Yes, they will," she retorted. "You really believe any of these people will clean up the kind of mess Buster makes?" Her logic was unassailable. Blowing her bangs out of her face, she pointed to the papers on the floor.

"Lessing's not unfamiliar with what comes out of the back end of a horse," he told her. "In fact, lawyers—as well as reporters—deal with the stuff all the time."

"And there's going to be a lot of it hitting the fan while they dicker over Buster," she argued. "My poor little guy. If Buster stays, I stay."

He gave in to the inevitable. "All right. Although you didn't have any trouble driving out of *my* life last night, did you?" His gaze remained steady on her face.

Unhappily, she began, "Mack—"

"Excuse me," interrupted Bess Tallart. For once her aura of polished superiority was missing. Her green eyes glistened . . . with tears.

Persephone didn't believe it was beyond Bess to conjure fake tears. But she respected the red tip of Bess's perfect nose, as well as the mascara streaks that gave Bess the sad eyes of a French clown doll. Persephone was certain that nothing but sincere emotional upset could get the *Portland Voice* reporter to reveal such cracks in her well-groomed facade.

Mack's glance grazed Bess. "What is it?"

Wincing at his impersonal tone—if Mack ever spoke to her like that, she would curl up and die—Persephone touched his arm. The least she owed him was a tactful retreat. "You two should talk in private. I'll go—"

Mack looked at her. "Still trying to run away?"

"Stay, please," Bess pleaded. "I owe you an apology as much as I owe one to Mack. I—uh—oh, God, this is hard." She stood first on one Italian pump, then on the other. "You hurt me, Mack. And the funny thing is, you didn't mean to. But you turned me down—right after you met Ms. Snow, evidently—and you showed you preferred her to me. Then you handed me the perfect opportunity to make a fool out of you. I took it. But I never foresaw that the whole situation would get so out of control. And I never, never imagined your unicorn might be real. Busteroo is so astonishing."

"Looks like a fat midget pony to me," Mack commented mildly.

He was going to play the scene with his former girl-friend light, Persephone realized.

She seconded his effort. "Mack, Buster's beautiful." She put a comforting arm around Bess's shoulders. "Even reporters fall under Buster's spell. Everybody does."

"All I said was—"

"Men can be so insensitive," Persephone said to Bess. "It's a gender thing."

"Mack was never exactly Prince Charming. He's a good man, though. The best. Take care of him, won't you?"

"That's up to Mack," Persephone replied in a low tone.

The glance she slid him wasn't as confident as she wished it would be. Everything about him looked good. His once-broken nose, his creased leather jacket, his sloping, powerful shoulders. She loved him so.

Was love enough? Was it ever enough? The force of hers made her skin hot, her mood fretful, her insides wobbly. Buster, currently slobbering over mint patties offered by Jeanette Lord, was going to be taken away from her. That fairy tale was ending. Was it possible for love to make her and Mack's fairy tale last a lifetime?

Unfortunately, even if Mack didn't hate her, his love must have gotten dented a bit in the wee hours of the morning.

His dark head turned in the direction of his own office. "Uh-oh. The serious players are disappearing behind closed doors."

Bess straightened into alert good posture. Letting her arm slip from the reporter's shoulder, Persephone jumped up and down. Her diminutive height made it impossible for her to see over the crowd that had shifted between them and Buster. "Do they have him? Mack, can you see?"

"Your pet? Yeah, Jeremy Lessing's leading him on the leash." A thoughtful narrowing of his eyes accompanied his sigh. "I suppose you want me to crash the meeting and get you in there."

"Absolutely," both women replied at once.

Mack pointed to Persephone. "You, yes." Turning to Bess, he hesitated. Maybe he wasn't Mr. Sensitivity, but he'd never had any desire to lacerate his ex-live-in's already wounded feelings.

Bess shrugged with would-be nonchalance. "I can tell when I'm being dumped. This time, anyway. I'll make it easy for you. Bye, both of you."

Mack smiled. "I always knew you had class."

As they turned toward his office, Persephone added, "Bess isn't the only one displaying class this morning."

"Thanks. Listen, here's what we're going to do. Just walk in like it would be a major mistake for anybody to throw you out."

"It would." Her delicate jaw was set at a determined angle.

"I knew you were a slugger. Let's go fight." He held open the door for her.

From where they stood, they had a clear view of Mack's office. Ganders was gesturing widely. The others—Lessing, Chasmo's rep and the university lawyer—were settling themselves in chairs and dragging papers out of briefcases. Seemingly forgotten, Buster lipped at a potted plant. His leash trailed on the floor, and his horn dug a small hole in the plaster wall.

Persephone went straight to the unicorn, tugging him after her into a straight-backed chair. With an audible sigh, Buster climbed into her lap.

Mack bent his head to hers. "Okay, explain to me what you want from this meeting."

She was busy stroking the critter's neck. "Hmm?"

"What's the best life you can visualize for Buster?" he rephrased. "Say it loud so everybody can hear."

Obediently, she raised her voice. "A good home. Plenty of room. Other minis to play with. The chance to reproduce naturally. A trainer who knows what he's doing—Buster deserves to be *seen*. He isn't a freak to be put into exploitation films. I've always believed he ought to be evaluated—but only by scientists who take into consideration the fact he's a living being, the only one of his kind. I mean, he's not a laboratory specimen to be autopsied and stuffed."

Just the thought of such a gruesome end caused her to wrap her arms around the beast.

Mack found himself wondering if she'd treat a human baby with the same unswerving devotion. He bet she would. The worrisome, nagging, tantalizing possibility he'd gotten her pregnant was never far from his mind. How could she have run . . .

Focusing back on the matter at hand—Buster—he crouched and patted the broad, hairy nose, just as he'd seen Persephone do. Buster seemed to like it. His wide lips wrinkled in an equine smile. His short chin lolled over Persephone's arm, and his eyes closed.

Mack measured the officials in the room with cynical eyes. "What do you say, folks?" he asked quietly. "I don't have to point out to anyone here the good sense of Ms. Snow's recommendations. She's a professional in animal care. In fact, right now she's the world's leading authority on the care and feeding of unicorns."

16

"YOU DID IT," said Persephone dazedly.

Mack drove his Lexus through early evening traffic, one hand on the steering wheel, the other firmly clasping her thigh. He wasn't sure she had noticed his grip. Persephone was very high on what had happened in his office.

"No, *you* did it." The soft dusk of autumn transformed the clutter of bridges crisscrossing Portland's skyline into a gilded cobweb.

"I never expected Buster's future to be settled so quickly. How did you get everybody to agree?"

"If you think that negotiation was hard, you ought to sit in on a boxing contract sometime. Piece of cake. What you need to negotiate are common interests or a lever. In this case, the common interest is the desire to avoid bad publicity. Chasmo can't afford it. You and I and Leo flat out don't want it."

"And the lever?" She leaned forward to stare out the windshield.

"You. You and Buster. You're the ones who made the deal click. Nobody could look at your baby snoring on your lap and not realize the cameras must have loved you. You think ol' Chasmo wants every animal lover on the planet to regard him as a villain?"

"He's never cared before. Uh, Mack, have you noticed—"

"That may be why his agent couldn't cut a deal with the university fast enough. Buster will board at the agricultural college and Chasmo's production company will have the rights to all film on him. Chasmo'll get half of all the profits the films make. The Ganders Busteroo Blue Home for Street Kids will get the other half. Buster will get a safe, spoiled, happy life. And assuming my bid on the castle has been accepted, we'll have us a building to renovate."

"It hasn't sunk in yet."

"You do look shell-shocked, princess." He let go of her thigh with a pat. Reaching for the cellular phone Persephone had returned to him, he punched out a number.

"I mean, I'm grateful neither of us will be going to jail," she said. "And I can see Buster whenever I want. It'll be better for him to get weaned from my presence slowly. They're having me make a tape of my voice he can listen to. After that I'll hit the vet's offices and the stables near Portland and see if I can find a job."

"Sounds good."

"Mack!" She was still looking out the window. "This isn't the bridge that leads to Laurelhurst."

"Damn. You're right." He talked into the phone. "Hi, Mom. Did you get the result on the bid for the castle? That so? Wait, is there someone else's voice in the background? *Who?*" Mack's mouth dropped open. "Yeah, I know you're of age, but…well, I hope you have a romantic evening, too. I guess."

Feeling stunned, Mack replaced the phone.

"Jeanette has a date?" Persephone asked.

"Yeah. A sleep-over date. With Joey."

"He seems pleasant," she said tentatively.

"Of course he's a great guy. It's just—he was talking about the woman he was seeing and he called her 'a hot widow.' I've never thought of my mother as a hot widow."

Persephone choked slightly. "Get used to it. She is. All right, so tell me."

"Tell you what?"

"The bid! Did you win the bid?"

"The state accepted my offer."

Crowing with triumph, Persephone latched on to his arm and hugged it. "You did it!"

"*We* did it." Mack gave her a slow smile. "We're going to have a shelter. I know I sounded confident, but I have to admit, now and then I had a few doubts. Somehow we won. It's a miracle."

"Don't underestimate yourself, as your mother would say." Sighing, she rested her head on his shoulder. "It didn't take a miracle. Just a little magic. By the way, *where* are you taking me?"

"Well, you have a choice here. You get to pick where we go."

His quick glance showed him that all the old wariness was creeping back into her eyes. "What's that mean?"

"I want you to fight for me." He returned his attention to the road. "You fought for Buster all along the line. A self-confessed coward like you. Now I want you to care enough about me to take some aggressive action."

"Mack, you know I love you."

"Prove it, princess."

"I *tried* to prove it. I tried to remove myself and all my messy problems from your life. You wouldn't have it. You—you used emotional blackmail to get me into your office this morning."

"It worked, too," he said with satisfaction.

"Well, let me tell you something. You were right, and I'm thrilled with the way things have turned out." Letting go of his leather sleeve, she crossed her arms over her chest and glared at him. "So what did you have in mind? As proof?"

"Interstate 5's coming up. Turn north, and we could drive to Seattle, take a few days' well-deserved vacation, maybe cruise the San Juans."

"In November?" In spite of the warm air blasting from the Lexus's heater, she shivered.

"I imagine we would find some way to keep warm. However, we also have the option of turning south. Sometime tomorrow, we'd get to Nevada. People get married without a wait in Nevada."

Her shivers changed into tingles of excitement.

"In other words, you want me to ask you to marry me," she said.

His harsh face was set in unreadable lines. "You got it."

"I'm not a maiden fair you rescued and got stuck with." She had to make sure he understood what he was suggesting. "You don't have to do this."

"Forgive me if I'm crude, but you're not a maiden at all anymore. Thanks to me, which is something I'm very happy about. Furthermore, I do not consider myself stuck with you. And I'm not doing the choosing here. You are. I-5 dead ahead. Which way will it be?"

"My father—"

"Somehow I knew we'd get back to him. Persephone, didn't you listen to my mom? There are rotten apples on everybody's family tree. Thomason Snow is just a bad memory. Like an evil spell. You broke the spell when you—*you*—decided the castle should be a shelter."

Rehashing the past was the only way she could think of to discover whether or not she and Mack had a future. "But the way he exploited women disgusts you. I couldn't bear it if you looked at me and thought of that."

"Where did you get the idea you are your father? When I look at you, I see you. Not him. Not his crimes. Hell, you're probably the biggest victim he ever had. And you survived. I know what surviving's all about. I didn't grow up in convent school. Boxing's not exactly a lily-white environment, either. This choirboy's reputation you seem to think I've got and you have to protect is a figment of your imagination." He spared her another glance. "Do you want me to tell you how proud I am of you again?"

She considered. "Yes, please."

"I'm proud of you. Damned proud."

"But people will never stop wondering if I have some of the loot from Daddy's prostitution ring salted away—"

"Sure they will. Especially when I sink a large chunk of my capital into buying your castle and you have to keep me on a stable hand's salary." He shrugged. "I can live with that. What I can't live with is the idea of losing you."

His steady gaze reminded her of the first time she'd ever seen him. The gray depths of his eyes had invited her to learn delights she'd never even imagined. And they still did.

The signboard for Interstate 5 rose up. "Well, Persephone?" asked Mack.

They came closer and closer. The Lexus passed the sign.

"We haven't even talked about married stuff," she said quickly. "I love working, but I also want babies. I think I have strong maternal instincts. Look how I flipped for Buster. Do you—"

"As far as I'm concerned, you can work as long as you like at whatever you like. And I want babies, too. When the time comes, we can figure out who stays home with them. Millions of couples do. Here's the turnoff. What's your pleasure, princess?"

"South!"

With skidding tires, the car sped toward Nevada.

A Note from Kelly Street

There are no rules in fairy tales.

Well, there are, but they're the topsy-turvy principles that guide magic . . . and those are the rules I used in *The Virgin & the Unicorn*. I'm not a rebel. Still, it was impossible to resist the lure of writing a book that would be a little risky, and truly out of the ordinary.

Temptation heroines are rarely virginal—Persephone Snow is a lady of the untouched, upper-crust variety. Heroes are by definition handsome—Mack Lord is a boxer, with a boxer's battered face and throaty voice.

How two such unlikely characters come to grips with the reality that they've fallen in love is the fun of the book. The fact that they are caretakers of a real, live unicorn makes this story their personal fairy tale.

There's magic all around us: the breathless excitement of a first kiss; the tender compromises (sometimes reached through fiery negotiation) necessary in a long-term marriage. Especially magical for me is how I can look at my husband of sixteen years and fall in love all over again.

I wish every reader the same sense of happily ever after.

I owe a debt of gratitude to Harlequin editors Birgit Davis-Todd, Malle Vallik and Susan Sopcek for letting me write *The Virgin & the Unicorn*. The opportunity to create a fairy tale was a dream come true for me.

And so was the thrill of breaking all the rules . . . just once.

Once upon a time...

THERE WAS A FABULOUS
PROOF-OF-PURCHASE OFFER
AVAILABLE FROM

As you enjoy your Harlequin Temptation LOVERS & LEGENDS stories each and every month during 1993, you can collect four proofs of purchase to redeem a lovely opal pendant! The classic look of opals is always in style, and this necklace is a perfect complement to any outfit!

One proof of purchase can be found in the back pages of each LOVERS & LEGENDS title...one every month during 1993!

LIVE THE FANTASY...

To receive your gift, mail this certificate, along with four (4) proof-of-purchase coupons from any Harlequin Temptation LOVERS & LEGENDS title plus $2.50 for postage and handling (check or money order—do not send cash), payable to Harlequin Books, to: **In the U.S.:** LOVERS & LEGENDS, P.O. Box 9056, Buffalo, NY 14269-9056; **In Canada:** LOVERS & LEGENDS, P.O. Box 621, Fort Erie, Ontario L2A 5X3.
Requests must be received by January 31, 1994.
Allow 4-6 weeks after receipt of order for delivery.

NAME: _____

ADDRESS: _____

_____

CITY: _____

STATE/PROVINCE: _____

ZIP/POSTAL CODE: _____

ACCOUNT NO.: _____

ONE PROOF OF PURCHASE   083 KAO